Nede Land 1: © 2020 by Yeral E. Ogando
The Hero Within - Volume Three
Publisher: Christian Translation LLC
Printed in the USA

This is a work of fiction. Names, characters, dialogue, places, and incidents are either a product of the author's imagination and are used fictitiously. Character's opinions are not necessarily the same as the authors. Any resemblance to persons living or dead is purely coincidental; they are not to be interpreted as real people or events.

ISBN 13: 978-1-946249-49-4

1. Series Fiction 2. Spiritual Warfare 3. Christian Fiction.

DEDICATION:

This book is dedicated to the unique and ever-lasting person who has always been there for me, no matter how stubborn I am:

GOD

I also want to dedicate this work to YOU (Rey Luis and Seferina), my beloved grandparents because without you, I would not be here. May you rest in peace with our Lord Jesus Christ in heaven! You were, and shall always remain, the best part of me.

I WILL ALWAYS LOVE YOU.

Always.

ACKNOWLEDGMENTS:

Thanks to God for allowing my dream to come true, and for giving me strength when I felt like giving up.

Had it not been for the support that I have received along the way from these incredible and amazing people, I would not be where I am today.

Thanks to my editor, Lucas Walsh for doing such a great job helping me polish this book.

And I can't forget to mention Hiraida Diaz for her continuous support and the brilliant ideas that she has contributed to The Hero Within series.

This has been a very long ride for my family, but the reward is worth the wait. Thanks to my daughters, Yeiris & Tiffany, and my sons Bennett, Ethan and Nathan for staying by my side through this journey. You know I love you.

Table of Content

CHAPTER 1

"For we wrestle not against flesh and blood, but against
principalities, against *powers*, against the *rulers of the darkness*
of this world, against *spiritual wickedness in high places*.
Ephesians 6:12"

When the *evil leaders* were in control of governing
the ghost towns, there was chaos and destruction.
People did not know why these cities were called
"ghost towns" even though they lived within them.
Nor did they know that these ghost towns were
strategically placed here on earth.

Anthony Markson was called by the *Holy Spirit,* or, as
He is called by His soldiers and disciples, *The Elite
Commander,* to seek out and locate normal people on
the edge of death. Anthony himself was called and
rescued from death to serve a higher cause for *The
Elite Commander.*

He was to rescue those without hope, bringing them
to the Lord, and lead them on an incredible quest.

By following the directions of *The Elite Commander,*
he started locating these people, but did not know at
that time that these people were going to be part of
an elite crew of warriors.

After being chosen, Anthony was given the name *"Warrior."* He fought evil entities and took part in many spiritual battles, enabling him to conquer each one of the new members of the team.

Endowed with a great power that was also a great burden, he started chasing after his targets with unrelenting persistence, locating them one by one. Fighting the demons that entangled their souls, and freeing them from their chains of slavery.

Once free, *The Elite Commander* started naming each new member, officially making them part of the ever-expanding team. Their continued search for others was accomplished with a higher purpose in mind.

As time passed by, eventually the team found and fostered, a lost soul called Erin Ludwig. Erin, a white female whose skin had yellow undertones, stood at around 5'7". She had lovely brown eyes with gold flecks and a heart-shaped face. She had a sharp, beautiful smile, and her body was sinewy and strong from daily work-outs, supported by willowy legs of solid muscle.

Erin was a nurse, but she would unknowingly become Anthony Markson's partner in future epic battles. Anthony Markson would soon be known as *Warrior,* and Erin would grow to become *Mender,* both names given to them by *The Elite Commander.*

But while working as a nurse in one of the local hospitals, Erin had already been fighting spiritually on her own. One day, when Anthony was visiting the hospital, attempting to locate one of his first targets, she saw a light in him that inspired her to call him "Brother."

A dangerous situation arose when a patient pulled a gun and threatened the other staff members. Erin was present, and she strongly encouraged the patient to hand over the weapon in Jesus's name.

Anthony was perplexed by the command in her voice and thought for a moment that Erin would make an excellent addition to the team; but he had yet to secure another member of the team that he was there fighting to save. After the incident, Anthony met Mr. and Mrs. Michael Reeves, for whose lives he would fight for as a warrior, bringing them to the Lord in the process.

When the team was almost complete, they received an order from *The Elite Commander* to secure six main ghost towns.

Each one of the towns was commanded by an evil leader and his associate. These two leaders were working for the great boss of evil, the one managing all the towns from an unknown location.

Each evil leader had a demon assigned to them, and although these demons were mere puppets in the kingdom of darkness, they were fully aware of their position, and took full advantage of the evil commander's lives. When the leaders needed more power they would call out to their demons, fusing with them, becoming something else, something very powerful; something ready to kill and destroy.

One day while on a non-authorized expedition into a ghost town called Slattersville, the team was rushed and decimated by the evil spirits governing the town. They ended up at the hospital where the nurse, Erin Ludwig, was working. Beaten and thrashed, the team conducted a prayer meeting in their hospital room, wherein *The Elite Commander* called Erin Ludwig to serve, changing her name to *Mender.* She was going to be part of the team. A team dedicated to fighting evil forces in spiritual realms, and demons that were visible to spiritual eyes only, and not to human eyes.

After their defeat, the team needed guidance and training in order to learn how to use their new spiritual powers bestowed upon them by The Lord, enhancing their ability to fight against demons and spiritual forces.

There was an ancient warrior watching them from a distance while they walked into a trap the evil spirits had prepared for them. This ancient warrior possessed an assortment of knowledge about spiritual battles and fighting demons. He had left that kind of life in the past after losing his whole family in an unexplainable accident. He knew it was evil forces that took his family, but he was compelled to put his weapon down for good.

His name was Daniel Samuels, or as he had been known back then, *The Emissary*. *The Elite Commander* called him back to work, to train the newly formed team of warriors, before they embarked on a great and dangerous adventure.

They were all trained by *The Emissary*, who taught them to use their new ability; the transformation technique that would turn them into *Knight Warriors* of *The Elite Commander*. In this state, they would receive Gifts of the Spirit, enabling them to fight battles and win them for the Lord.

After their training was completed, *The Elite Commander* paired the team members and sent them into the six towns to conquer and deliver them from the hands of evil leaders and commanders. These six towns were placed strategically across the state of Ohio, effectively keeping it under the reign of evil.

The Elite Commander paired Anthony Markson, who had become known as *Warrior* with Erin Ludwig, who was now known as *Mender,* and sent them into the town of Knockemstiff. *Mender's* power is represented by the number 8, which she often keeps it concealed from others because it presents her as weaker than most of the other members of the team.

They were ordered to fight the evil leader *Assassin* and his associate *Poisson Dagger.*

Assassin, once known as *Koroshiya San,* was the strongest ranked, at #1, among the evil commanders. He towered above all other men and his voice resounded as thunder when he taunted and mocked his opponents. He was brash and irreverent, taking great pride in his strengths and abilities to strike terror into the hearts of his enemies. His one goal was conquest. His demon is called *Malphas,* and when fused together, they are practically invincible.

The second in command at Knockemstiff is *Poisson Dagger,* who is also known as Garnet Dukes. A Spanish descendant and samurai warrior raised in Japan, Dukes entered the States, immediately establishing his legacy as a ruthless and cruel individual with a heart that was hardened against all things good and decent. He fuses himself with the demon named *Eligos*. He ranks at number 7 in power. As it is with the *Warriors*, the lower the number of their rank, the stronger the demon.

Warrior and *Mender* were sent to conquer Knockemstiff, and they fought in great battles. In the end, they used their special training to win the spiritual battle and triumph over the evil forces. The two evil leaders, *Assassin,* his demon, *Malphas*, and *Poisson Dagger* and his demon, *Eligos*, were defeated.

The town now belongs to the Lord and the conquerors of the ghost town were *Warrior* and *Mender.* They became *The Evangelism Team* while working on this town, preaching and healing others with the help of the two warriors and their gifts.

Knockemstiff was a somber town, one that nobody wanted to enter without proper introduction. The lurking darkness surrounding the town had turned it into a ghost town. Most of the people, the good people, left the town a long time ago, and now only a few good ones remained. They felt a deep loyalty to Knockemstiff because it was the town of their ancestors. Most of the other remaining population were stricken with a love of vice and evil, and were controlled by demon forces and evil spirits.

It was a land of nobodies, but there was something hidden in the town as well, something that no one except one man was aware of.

"*Warrior*," said Mender, very concerned, "We have been preaching and teaching for a long time in this town with most of the people coming to the Lord; but still, whenever one pronounces the town's name, Knockemstiff, it sounds as if darkness itself were vocalized. I think we should pray about this name and see what The Elite Commander has to say. What do you think?"

"Well, actually, I have been thinking about that very thing lately." replied *Warrior*. "I remember that, when the Lord calls someone, He changes his name into something excellent, like how I became *Warrior*. Remember reading in the Bible how the Lord changed the names of evil ones, cheaters, and wrongdoers into something special?

Warrior continued, "I also remember the case of Abram, for when the Lord God Almighty changed his name into Abraham, it was a glorious sign of his ascension. I think the same thing needs to happen with this city. Let us discuss it with *The Evangelism*

Team later, but in the meantime let us pray about this name."

When they approached *The Evangelism Team*, told them of their concerns about the name of the town, they all began thinking about the meaning of that name. They became convinced it should be changed, but praying was the only way to get true answers and anything done in this town now. Before, it was evil, and now it is about lifting up in prayer, because the team of *The Elite Commander* is present.

CHAPTER 2

"But the fruit of the Spirit is love ... Galatians 5:22-23"

Whenever the residents of Knockemstiff mention the name of the town, it would resurrect and empower the negative vibes left behind by its previously slain demons, *Malphas* and *Eligos*. The residents knew the name of the town was a favorite among demons and evil commanders.

When the entire *Evangelism Team*, along with Anthony and Erin, started praying about the name of the town, they became steeped in the spirit, their vision purified, and even the air itself seemed to shimmer with the spirit. Their minds raced and were filled with scrambled letters like the pages of a codebook being turned over by a cryptographer. At last, when they were all as one, *The Elite Commander* revealed the new name of the town, and it was made using the same letters. It was incredible! Knockemstiff's new name was Mock Fenk Fist. The team was reluctant at first, not fully understanding the true meaning behind the new name, but had faith there was something powerful about it, since *The*

Elite Commander Himself had given the order to change it.

Evil forces could no longer control Mock Fenk Fist, and when the citizens of the town heard the new name, they did not understand it either. They found humor in the fact that the team turned the old name into a new one without even changing a single letter. Nevertheless, they rejoiced in Mock Fenk Fist, because the town was now governed and ruled by God fearing people.

The other five cities were also conquered and eventually ruled over by each assigned pair of *The Evangelism Team*, as follows:

Slattersville would be ruled by *Judge* and *Discerner*, while Moonville would come under the protection of *Psychic* and *Marvel. Newville* was *Decipher* and *Polyglot's* domain, and Blue Ball was guarded and ruled by *Shrewder* and *Faith Woman*. Lastly, Hell Town was conquered by *The Emissary.*

Pastor Good came from New York when called by Janet Markson, who was giving him updates about her new experience in Ohio. Not knowing exactly what was going on, he needed to head to Ohio with *The Evangelism Team,* because he felt the Lord was pulling him there for a mission. A very charismatic leader, Pastor Good was filled with the Spirit of the Lord; he was always quick to answer any call he received to evangelize or build a new church.

He arrived in Ohio, taking Janet and the team by surprise. He was taken aback himself, though, when he learned of some of the work the team had been doing and how much he was needed. Immediately, they started analyzing and delegating functions for each town. First, they were to build a new church in each of the six towns. The Pastor wasn't sure how he was going to manage six churches, but he had *The Evangelism Team* with him. With their help, and most of all, the help of the Lord God Almighty, he knew he would be able to accomplish anything.

He decided to supervise the work going on in each town, and thus, decided to take up residence in Hell Town, as it was more centrally located. Starting with weekly trips to preach and teach the Bible, as well as cultivating discipleship where it was needed, through his hard work, the Pastor was happy to serve the Lord. He prayed hard for guidance, for he still lacked confidence in his ability to set up and lead these six new churches.

• • • • • • • • ••

One day the team decided to take an excursion to some remote areas of the town, those areas that people normally do not travel to or settle down in. There had been reports of troubling riots in those areas over the last few weeks, and *Warrior* thought it was time to investigate.

"I think it is time for us to visit the troublesome areas of this town," remarked *Mender*, "I have been getting disturbing reports from those areas and we cannot allow a few ruffians to disturb the peace we have worked so hard to establish for the citizens of this town."

Warrior had some of the same concerns. "Let us pray about it along with *The Evangelism Team*, and tomorrow we will head to those areas." He continued cautiously, "We have conquered the town Knockemstiff and renamed it Mock Fenk Fist. Even though we still don't understand the meaning of the name, we must make all the inhabitants proud of the change."

"After all," *Warrior* continued, "We are working for *The Elite Commander*, and we cannot allow disturbances of this kind."

After praying for a few hours, they finally received confirmation that they should visit those areas the very next day. So, *Warrior* and *Mender* set out on their way to the troublesome areas post haste. Their orders were to go alone and inspect the areas before taking *The Evangelism Team* to finish the work they would start.

When *Warrior* and *Mender* made it to the specified zone, they were speechless. The scene was utterly shocking, and compared to the rest of the town, this was positively hellish. The population in these areas were filled with perversion, debauchery and vileness. It was an entirely alien-like world, filled with sickness, death and decay. It appeared as though this area of town had been wholly unaffected by the team's victory over Mock Fenk Fist.

"How can this be? I cannot believe my eyes. What is going on here?" *Mender* was speaking herself into an almost shocked silence.

"It *appears evil* has moved from the main area of the town to the outskirts, but I thought these areas were not inhabited. The tales I was hearing did not even come close to describing the state of things." *Warrior* replied.

Even the breeze was stale and heavy while the whole landscape was somber, as if something evil was controlling everything and weighing it down. But neither *Warrior* nor *Mender* could sense or see any focal point of evil in those areas.

"*Warrior*," said *Mender* solemnly, "You have received the Gift of Goodness, and that is something these people could use right about now."

"You are right, *Mender.*"

Clearing his throat, *Warrior* continued. "And you can use the Gift of Hearing that was bestowed upon you. Let us head home and bring *The Evangelism Team* into action." After pausing momentarily, *Warrior* finished speaking with a defiant thought.

"We will accompany them to fight for this part of town. We must conquer and free these people."

• • • • • • • ••

They headed back home, and once there, they shared all the details of their excursion with *The Evangelism Team* and Pastor Good, who had been spending a few days there to supervise the operation.

"Let us take the team to this part of the town tomorrow evening," Pastor Good said after *Warrior* and *Mender* had concluded their report. "We will minister to the people for three days in a row, and bring them to the Lord!" All that were present cheered in agreement.

He went on, "Anthony and Erin, you do what you need to do, and we will accompany you as ministers to these people."

They both nodded stoically. Even though Pastor Good was working directly with the Warrior Team, he could not yet fully understand the magnitude of the spiritual work *Warrior* and *Mender* were *taking on*. Since he was not part of the *Warrior Team* himself, he could not see the spiritual realm nor fight in battles like *Warrior* or *Mender*.

The next evening, the entire *Evangelism Team* and Pastor Good were back in the outskirts of town ministering to the people. While preaching the sermon, *Warrior* and *Mender* could sense a heavy, evil atmosphere touching the congregation. It was as if some invisible force was coming down from above, and they knew something was amiss. They finished the first night's ministry without one citizen coming to the Lord, even after a powerful message from Pastor Good. During the afternoon, *The Evangelism Team* visited each family one by one and invited them to witness the three days of service.

"Anthony, I believe you and Erin should minister tomorrow after the service," advised Pastor Good,

"This crowd is tough, and I believe they are here just for the food supply, but we can use that to our advantage. Let us win them." He was smiling warmly while wrapping Anthony on the shoulder.

On the second day of service, the crowd had increased in number, and about a hundred people were now gathered. They were drunken and smelled of sin, especially the hungry ones. The vices of the town had overtaken them and it was impossible to hide. It was obvious even from a distance that these people were enslaved by their vices, and that they needed salvation more than ever, but something or *someone* was holding them back from Christ.

The first day, *The Evangelism Team* gave out the entire food supply, and more than half of the crowd disappeared. They decided on the second day to give out the food and first aid supplies *after* the service, to see if that changed the outcome at all.

Indeed the sermon was one of a kind and touched the hearts of many gathered there. In fact, Erin herself was so moved that she could barely see through the tears in her eyes. When the time came for ministering, Anthony and Erin started their task by waving their hands in the air and placing them upon the people who came forward. Erin was praying for healing and wanted to pass it along to the people, but somehow, it was not working. The people were not receiving any healing miracles. Anthony continued to ask for goodness to touch their lives and hearts, *but still saw no changes.* The powerful hand of *The Elite Commander* did not appear to be working on them.

They readied themselves to fight battles for these people, and the Lord, but there was no sign of a visible enemy. What could they do? They could not even transform themselves into their warrior or knight forms because there was not a visible enemy to fight. *Something* beyond their sight was happening and they needed to figure it out.

CHAPTER 3

" *"But the fruit of the Spirit is... Joy ... Galatians 5:22-23""*

Seeing the hardness and hardship of the people those first two days, the team decided to dedicate the last full day of the ministry to the Bible, Praying and Fasting, or as they liked to call it, BPF. They wanted to intercede in the spiritual affairs of these people, hoping for results like they had seen in all the other parts of the town. They wanted to see the powerful hand of *The Elite Commander*, but somehow they were not seeing it working in this part of the town.

Pastor Good looked to *Warrior* and *Mender* and spoke. "While you two are ministering in tonight's service, we will stand by you, creating a powerful prayer ring. We want to see the miracle of healing and goodness in these people with the hands of The Lord God Almighty backing us up tonight." They all agreed.

As the night descended, the team began to minister to the crowd. People from other parts of the town began flooding in, until there were more than three hundred gathered. People had heard about the service and decided to go and support the teams. They have enjoyed their Gifts of Healing, and they wanted to see others touched by them as well.

Pastor Good was a very exceptional man. He was incredibly wise and eloquent with his words. Listening to his sermons could make you feel like a sharp sword was going through your bones, touching the most inner parts of your soul, and yet, the people of this zone remained unaffected.

There was a small family of three living in the outskirts of the town. They did not come to the service the first or second night, but they were present for the last night of the event. They did not come for food or first aid kits; they wanted to hear the people giving the sermons that everyone was talking about.

Out of the three members of that family, one was very ill. The mother had been suffering with a chronic skin disease and they did not know how to cure her; she lost an arm the year before because of this terrible disease.

Inspired by others, they came hoping to hear the Word of God. They hoped beyond hope to find a miracle. The family had been suffering for a long time and they had tried everything from doctors to witch doctors, witchcraft and magic, and nothing had been able to heal their mother.

People say that they were once a wealthy family, but once the disease touched the mother's skin, they spent everything they had trying to find a cure, with no success. There were times when the mother of this family wished she was dead in order to relieve her son and daughter of the terrible burden she had become.

But her son and daughter loved her unconditionally, and they would never give up on her. When the time came for the sermon and Pastor Good was inspired and determined to transmit the presence of the Holy Spirit through his words. The message that evening was one of hope and healing, one of goodness and forgiveness, and people began to sob while the words flowed from his mouth. *The Evangelism Team* was praying as well, which added to the spiritual potency. Warrior and Mender were on guard, praying and ready for any eventuality. They felt the ever present somberness in the air that remained, even on the third day of the event. Sometimes, they felt like it was hard to pray because of the thickness in the air.

Pastor Good finished his sermon and that was the signal for Warrior and Mender to minister. The pair stepped out onto the stage, opened their spiritual eyes and what happened next was truly a sight to behold.

A dark cloud appeared, hovering over the whole area, sinister and not of this world. Reacting to this evil presence, *Warrior* and *Mender* transformed into their fighting form while still ministering to the people.

"*Mender!*" Shouted *Warrior,* "What is this dark cloud? I sense something evil coming out of it, but I cannot see anything!"

Amid a tempest that had begun swirling around the cloud, *Mender* replied, "Even if we are ready to fight, the enemy is not of this world and we cannot see it! We must do something drastic!"

At this very moment, the woman who had long suffered from that awful disease passed by *Mender*. She instantly felt a draining on her spirit that shot out of her and touched someone unknown in the crowd. It was the first time in the whole sermon that she had felt her power disperse and heal someone.

Warrior and *Mender* finished ministering amid the winds and shadows, yet the dark cloud persisted. They were the only ones who could see it, of course. Pastor Good and *The Evangelism Team* could feel the heaviness in the atmosphere, but could not see or perceive the dark cloud.

At the end of the services there was a report that a family of three came to the Lord.

The mother stepped up, speaking to *Warrior* and *Mender*. "I have been suffering for many years, trying everything to cure myself, but nothing helped. When we heard about your God and the things He was doing within the town, I felt some hope for the first time in a long while."

The woman stretched out her arm to show *Mender* that she had but one remaining. *Mender* felt the suffering of this woman, and she finally understood where her power had gone during their ministry. The woman was not yet healed, but she, her son and daughter had given their lives to Christ.

The woman continued saying, "I have given my life to the Lord today. Although, I am not sure what is going to happen, I feel content for the first time in years. Whether the disease is still present or not, my heart is now as clean as the driven snow."

Mender prayed and the skin of the woman began to ripple and change until it was covered in healthy, new flesh, as clean as the day she was born. The woman received the Gift of Healing, and was now a changed woman, one of the Lord's children. The crowd knew the woman and her family well, and they all rejoiced, even though some of the people were secretly jealous.

The miracle of healing was present at that exact moment. *Warrior* picked his timing and said to the woman, "Woman, you have given your life to Christ and are now a renewed person in your heart and soul, now let us make everything new in you." Looking at *Mender*, he made a small gesture, telling her to touch the place where the woman's arm had been. *Mender* did so, and the woman's lost arm was restored at that very moment.

The Gift of Goodness and Healing touched this family and yet none of the other members of this small community were touched by the power of *The Elite Commander.*

The team finished handing out the food supplies with the help of the new believers, including the newly restored woman, who amazed the people by her very presence. To think that not only ten minutes ago this woman who was an amputee in the midst of great agony, was now serving them food from both hands. What a miracle!

There were no more reports of conversions or healing miracles, but everyone on the team was happy. They knew there was a party in heaven for these three souls that had come to serve Christ. Yet, *Warrior* and *Mender* were still deep in thought about the dark power hovering around the zone.

"*Mender*, I think we should investigate further into this dark cloud matter. We should dedicate some time to BPF and seek answers from *The Elite Commander.*" said *Warrior* emphatically.

"Yes, I agree that we should spend some time reading the *bible, praying* and *fasting* on this matter. Starting tomorrow, if that is ok with you. Should we invite the others, or should we do it alone?" asked *Mender* thoughtfully.

Warrior's words spoke true. "I think this is something you and I must handle alone. The others can't comprehend this matter because they still cannot see this dark cloud. Let us ask them to continue praying instead, for the souls that did not come to the Lord."

"Agreed."

"

CHAPTER 4

*But the fruit of the Spirit is...**Peace** ... Galatians 5:22-23"*

"There is imminent danger in that part of town. I could feel the evil presence during the three days of services, but I did not see anything."

Warrior continued, imploring in humble supplication.

"Speak to us and reveal your purpose in this matter. The dark cloud hovering over those people, giving off dense vibes, is something out of the ordinary. We have not seen anything like it before. Speak to us today, Lord God Almighty."

Together they prayed, "We are gathered here as your servants and warriors and you are our *Elite Commander.* Holy Spirit, manifest yourself and let us know thy will."

"The people need healing, and some goodness Father God, please send your Holy Spirit to shine upon them, using us as your vessels for this purpose." *Warrior* and *Mender* continued praying without having any clear response from God, *The Elite Commander.*

The team spent a full day of BPF with no directional response, but they knew their continued prayers were heard; they just needed to wait for the truth to be revealed to them.

"*Warrior,*" Mender spoke with conviction, "Now that I think about it, the evil presence felt more like that of *Malphas* and *Eligos.* Those two demons that were tormenting this town before us. We have defeated them and their human puppets, *Assassin* and *Poisson Dagger.* What we felt *today is similar but far* greater in strength. We *need to stay vigilant for something evil is approaching, we just don't have clear vision just yet.*"

Warrior listened intently as she carefully added, "We know that part of the town is lost in lasciviousness, deprivation and sickness. Something powerful is affecting these people."

In the middle of the night, Pastor Good was having a bad dream. It started out on a bright day and the team was praying. Suddenly, out of nowhere, someone approached and spirited *Warrior* and *Mender* away.

The following day Pastor Good relayed his dream to *Warrior* and *Mender,* "I could not see where you were taken, but I have a very strange feeling about it. I could not sleep after that." Gravely Pator Good continued, "I prayed for the interpretation of the dream, but the Lord is quiet. I wanted to share this uneasy feeling with you both, especially since the dream was about you." After he spoke, the three of them continued sitting together, but in silence.

• • • • • • • • •

A few weeks passed by without any response from *The Elite Commander*, and feelings among the group were still uneasy. They could not fathom why the people in this small community were not influenced at all by the power of Healing and the Gift of Goodness. There were clearly dark forces hindering the blessings presented to the townsfolk, but completely a mystery as to where it was coming from. They were in urgent need of healing and goodness, but *Warrior* and *Mender*'s power was not strong enough to reach them; they needed a miracle and fast.

"Be vigilant and ready. A new quest is approaching and you will need to be stronger than ever. A threat, not of this world, is approaching this town. Be ready. You must find it."

The Elite Commander's message was cryptic, giving no explanation of what they should expect. It ended as abruptly as it came. Although the team was clearly confused, they understood something evil was approaching, and they needed to be ready for it. Could the impending battle be with the malicious *Assassin* and *Poisson Dagger,* since they were nowhere to be found. They quickly vanished after being defeated by *Warrior* and *Mender.*

The town needed protection and saving from the approaching dark cloud. They knew a loss would only mean trouble, and more darkness for everyone.

"Could it be that we will battle evil forces once more in order to win this town for Christ?" inquired *Warrior.*

Mender's voice cracked as she spoke. "I don't know, but whatever is coming is strong, and we need to fight harder than ever, if we expect to defeat it." Looking directly into *Warrior*'s eyes, she continued, "*The Elite Commander* specifically said that the threat coming to this town was not of this world. We will be facing powerful evil spirits soon. We just don't know if they will be in their human or evil spirit forms. We must be ready."

. . . .

There was something lurking in the dark whenever the team members moved around the other five towns. While performing miracles, healings and assisting other brothers in preaching, they could sense a sidelong, fading look mingled within the shadows of the crowds.

The team seemed not to notice, since it was so subtle, choosing to ignore it. After defeating gigantic evil leaders, impressive commanders and conquering the Six Cities, this seemed almost a flutter in the wind.

Anthony Markson called an emergency meeting with all the team members currently located in the other towns, Pastor Good and *The Evangelism Team* as well.

"Pastor Good, would you honor us with a prayer to start the e-meeting?" asked Anthony, in a polite manner.

"Certainly, it would be my great pleasure," he answered. "Let us all close our eyes and raise our voices to heaven."

"Heavenly Father, we are gathered here today as your humble vessels. Use us, guide us and instruct us

according to thy will. In Jesus Almighty's name we pray, Amen!"

Anthony started sharing with the brothers their most recent experience at the outskirts of Mock Fenk Fist, and how frustrated they felt with the dark cloud. After he finished reporting, he gave the floor to Pastor Good who had raised his voice, asking for the opportunity to speak.

"Anthony, I did not see the dark cloud you mentioned, but I could sense a powerful evil spirit in the air. The way we ministered and preached to this crowd, I was expecting more conversions and healing miracles." After pausing briefly, he continued, "I understood that the dark presence I was feeling somehow had something to do with it and with your report, I am one hundred percent sure that there is something evil approaching. Brothers, we need to continue preaching. We need to reach every single soul in these towns. Our goal is to share the Word of Salvation and make disciples out of them. I am sure the Lord will do the rest." Pastor Good projected with fervor. They all said "Amen," together in reverence to God Almighty.

The other members reported sharing a more subtle, yet evil presence, in their respective towns as well.

They hadn't realized the heaviness in the air was gaining traction. They all agreed to spend more time in BPF, seeking answers and guidance from the Lord.

The team was about to close the meeting with a prayer and when Erin's voice spoke up. "Brothers, there is something else I would like to report on: Somehow Anthony forgot a very important part of the message, but that is why we are a team." Anthony looked surprised, not knowing what he had forgotten. Erin told everyone about Pastor Good's dream. Everyone paid close attention to the description of the dream, but no one offered any interpretation at all. The part that grabbed their attention the most, however, were the words *not of this world*. Daniel Samuels, the teacher of the group, had remained in complete silence during this little lecture. Anthony had taken notice and inquired, "Brother Daniel, do you want to say something to the group? You seem off today."

"I have been listening to all of you and I would like to request the opportunity to close the meeting with prayers." He said, soberly.

"By all means, if no one has anything else to say today," paused Anthony, "Brother Daniel Samuels will guide us in prayer." They all agreed.

Unbeknownst to the team there was a secret hidden in the depths of Daniel Samuels' heart. *The Emissary*, as he was called, knew it was not yet time to share it with the other warriors. They were not ready; they had too much work to do. Baby steps.

CHAPTER 5

" *But the fruit of the Spirit is... Longsuffering ... Galatians 5:22-*

23"

After several months of spiritual warfare, the results were incredible. They had started setting up the churches in each town. In some of the towns, the Gifts of the Spirit bestowed upon the warriors were very visible in the signs and miracles performed in their journeys. But Anthony and Erin were not very pleased at all with the outskirts of Mock Fenk Fist. They were continuously infested with evil and the dark cloud was getting even scarier. It was somehow spreading to other areas of the town as well. Something needed to be done urgently.

That is when Anthony received a call from Daniel Samuels requesting a meeting with *The W*arrior Team. There was something urgent in his voice, and it was time for *Warrior* and *Mender* to hear some good news, or so they thought.

"Praise the Lord," said *The Emissary*, "we are gathering here today for this e-meeting because there are important matters to discuss and share with you all." Everybody looked surprised. "Before starting, as the team leader Anthony, would you lead us in prayer?"

"My pleasure." replied Anthony. After finishing his prayer, he said, "Daniel, you called the meeting, you are the lead today."

"Very well then. Brothers, we are gathered here today at *Hont Well...*" He trailed off, "I beg your pardon, this is an e-meeting, and I am not used to this."

"You forgot the name of the town?" Warrior inquired.

"It may look that way, but I have not forgotten," said The Emissary, "allow me to explain so that you may understand."

Without hesitation he continued, "Pastor Good, *The Evangelism Team* and I thought it was time to change the name of *this* city from Hell Town to Hont Well City. We prayed for a new name, and God revealed that if we scrambled the old name in a specific way, an incredible meaning would be reveal itself. If you look carefully, it has the same letters as the old name, but we transformed it, and God gave it real meaning. Praise the Lord!" Everybody was glad and surprised at the same time.

That was also the case, of course, with Mock Fenk Fist, but the other members followed with similar statements about changing their towns names too.

"All the towns now carry new names. Praise the Lord! This is incredible," exclaimed *The Emissary*, "Even when we were far away from one another, we were one in spirit." He was bursting with joy and reverence for God.

They all rejoiced, praising and worshiping the name of the Lord God Almighty, for all of the battles they had won, the people that came to the Lord, and the improvements made to each of the cities.

Daniel Samuel, better known as *The Emissary,* is in charge of Hont Well City. He cleared his throat, and in a gravely, serious tone, began to speak.

"All of you have grown and matured in all ways these past months. We now have instructions to fortify the work in our respective towns, because there is a great danger lurking in the shadows. We may have winning these battles, but the war is far from over."

"As you know, we have found several of the evil human leaders. They have few memories of what has transpired. For them, it has been like a dream, but we all know the truth. We need to work hard, making sure each one of them serves the Lord." He continued after a short pause, "Or, I am afraid the consequences will be devastating for their souls and for each one of our cities."

Warrior stepped forward to speak, "During these past few weeks, I have been sensing a fading, subtle evil lurking in the shadows, but I admit to not paying it much attention. However, the dark cloud I spoke about in the previous meeting *is* getting worse, and it is expanding to other *areas of Mock Fenk First.* Now, I will open my eyes, and pay much more heed, for I fear that its strength is growing." All the team members agreed to do the same.

"As a final word for this meeting," said *Warrior,* "I tell you that there is something divine behind why we are working on each town. Whatever the reason, there is something powerful and precious conducting all of this. I know it was not a coincidence, or chance *The Elite Commander* chose these cities. I don't believe in coincidences but in God-incidences. I am absolutely certain there is a great plan, and great deeds for us still to accomplish. We might have to battle soon."

"Has the Lord spoken to you, *Warrior?*" asked *The Emissary.*

"The only words I have received from *The Elite Commander* are the ones Erin shared in our previous meeting," answered *Warrior*, "But since the dark cloud is spreading, I believe evil is fast approaching."

That is when *The Emissary* took the floor and said, "I agree, we still don't know, but there is another matter at hand."

"I have found some old books and I think there is something more in them than meets the eye."

They all looked at each other, hesitantly.

"Old books..." *Warrior* repeated.

"Try searing for books," The Emissary explained, "Recovering any that might call your attention. Ancient and forgotten books in your towns. Pray for the Lord's guidance in your search."

He spoke reassuringly, "There is something we must know, and it is hidden within these book's pages, of which I speak."

The members of the team did not know how to respond to this last statement, remaining calm, yet uneasy.

Daniel Samuels said, "Let us pray before departing. Erin, would you do us the honor of praying?"

"Any time, Emissary," said Erin, "Let us close our eyes in reverence to our Lord God Almighty."

"Abba, Father." Erin, raising her voice, spoke so all could hear.

"We humbly come to You seeking Your guidance. We are thankful for everything You have done for us, and for all You will do for us in the future. We know that the battles we've won, were won because *You* fought for us and with us. Lord, we've prayed, and You have not answered. We are facing something unknown to us but not to You. We need Your guidance, Lord. You placed us here in these cities for Your work to be done. Please, don't mute your ear to us now, Lord! Let Your will be done! Amen!"

With this, they all concluded the meeting with their minds uneasy and thoughtful. "Ancient books, forgotten books…" The words echoed amid their thoughts as they walked.

CHAPTER 6

*" "But the fruit of the Spirit is... **Kindness** ... Galatians 5:22-23"*

"*Mender*, there must be a meaning to the new name of the town." said Warrior. "Let us pray and search for the meaning of the name we received for this town, Mock Fenk Fist." *Mender* chided out in laughter.

"I thought the name sounded funny, but I did not want to say anything at first, but I only slightly mocked the name. I understand now why you always use the initials "MFF" when referring to the name of the city. At first, I thought you were confused and trying to say "BFF"."

"Hilarious," laughed *Warrior*, "You are indeed my best friend forever, but I was just avoiding saying Mock Fenk Fist. I know it sounds like a weird name, but I prefer it to Knockemstiff." They both laughed. *Warrior* and *Mender* were still unable to locate the evil leaders, *Assassin* and *Poisson Dagger*.

"Can we continue our search?" asked *Mender* reflectively.

"Wait, but we haven't even started. How can we continue?" said *Warrior.*

"*Warrior*, I was talking about our search to find the evil leaders, *Assassin* and *Poison Dagger.*"

"Ah! You got me there, *Mender.* It's been over a year and we still haven't been able to locate them. They cannot have vanished; the other teams have located their evil leaders." *Mender* despaired.

There was a pause. "It feels weird not to use our hero names, eh?" *Warrior* giggled.

"Yes, it has been a long time. We should stick to our new names then." *Mender* said, in a resolute tone.

"Agreed." They said in unison.

• • • • • • • •

Frantic and horrid feelings completely overtook *Warrior*, making him open his eyes and shoot up, rigid with fear from his fitful sleep. The same nightmare again.

"I do not understand it." He gasped, wiping cold sweat from his brow.

"Wait," he whispered confusedly, "I just closed my eyes for 5 minutes and I had that dream again. I will have to speak with *Mender* tomorrow; I am starting to have uneasy feelings, and the Lord is not speaking to me about it either."

"Knock, knock!" A desperate and hoarse whisper sprang from behind the door. "*Warrior!*"

Warrior, not recognizing the voice at first, replied, "What is happening? Is everything ok, *Mender*?"

"Yes, but I feel disturbed. I just had a nightmare."

When *Warrior* opened the door, *Mender* came bursting in, and before he could even utter a word, she started pouring her heart out to him, at a rapid and unnerving pace.

"I saw myself in a different town, but it felt familiar, as if I knew it very well. I can't quite remember it, but it was a different town, that's for certain." She was pacing the room, waving her arms, as if trying to conjure the town out of thin air.

"There was an enormous battle and..." her voice trembled and trailed off, "I lost against *Assassin* and

Poisson Dagger. I cannot describe the feeling, but I am terrified." She whipped around to face *Warrior.*

"I'm freaking out here! I don't want to close my eyes! It felt so vivid, like it was real. It's like I can literally feel the pain of the wounds crawling over my body." She sank onto the floor, exhausted from the effort.

"Hey, calm down, it was just a nightmare," soothed Warrior, "Take a deep breath, relax. Let us pray to sooth our nerves."

They prayed to the Lord God Almighty, and *Mender* was able to relax, but still felt uneasy.

"You know, I was going to talk to you about it tomorrow," said *Warrior*, "But I have been having a weird and terrifying dream too. The same dream again and again. I see you lying on the ground and I see someone that looks like *Assassin* and *Poisson Dagger* hurting you. They are saying things to you that I cannot understand. I try to help you but as soon as I reach out, I wake up." He sounded angry, and frustrated with himself.

"I have prayed, but I still don't have an answer," he continued, "Let us pray together, *Mender.* I still don't know what all of this means, but we will find out soon enough. It is…creepy that we're having the same dream, especially since we have already defeated them once before. I know we haven't found them yet, but still, could it be that we will fight them again and lose?" *Warrior* finished, looking tired.

"I cannot believe that the Lord hasn't talked with either of us about it," said *Mender*, "Let us pray."

They both prayed together for wisdom, understanding and the interpretation of the dream.

• • • • • • • •

Meanwhile, Anthony's wife and son Ben were settling into the new town. Ben had already made some new friends, and they had decided to play outside for a little bit. While walking in the neighborhood, they noticed an old abandoned building not far from his house. All the kids were in awe, staring at the old, creepy looking structure. It looked like it used to be some kind of library. Ben's eyes glimpsed something that looked like the corner of an old book, and he immediately felt like a gravitational pull towards it. He could not understand why, but this old book was somehow appealing to him. He grabbed for the old book but realized it was underneath a pile of junk.

He unrumpled the area to better reach the book. As he was grasping for the leather cover, he felt someone, or *something,* big coming towards him. He saw two big feet in front of him, but he just froze, unable to look up, or speak. He *tried* to move with all his will, but his body was not responding. The other kids didn't seem to notice anything strange, and were calling out to Ben, but he couldn't respond. Then, one of them went to him and said, confusedly, "Ben come on, let go of that thing. Let's get out of this spooky building. It just gives me the creeps." Suddenly, Ben snapped out of it, and without hesitation, turned and ran out of the building.

The force inside the building was unaware that Ben had seen it.

While Ben was walking back home with his friends, he was thoughtful, not speaking a word along the way. While his friends were talking with one another about all the cool things they'd seen, Ben couldn't utter a word in reply, he was too deep in his thoughts. He flashed back to a time when he was sick at the hospital. He once had a vision of his dad in shiny armor, fighting a dark force in the hospital room with him. He thought, *Could this be the same entity?*

He wasn't *entirely sure,* but he felt strongly that the two were connected somehow.

· · · · · · · · ·

"Dad, look what I found," said Ben, upon returning home, "It's very dusty and old. Can you read it to me, Dad?"

"Let me have a look at this *old and dusty* book." His father replied, taking the book from his son's hands. Anthony, a strong, intelligent fellow, was perplexed when he examined the book. Then, perplexity turned into astonishment. He could not believe his eyes, and it showed on his face.

"Dad…Dad, are you ok?" asked Ben.

"Yes, buddy, I'm fine. Go uh…go see your mother and ask if she needs help with that project she's been working on. I will join you shortly."

"Ok, Daddy. Can I have the book back?" Ben asked hesitantly.

"Well, I will give it back to you later on. I want Erin to see it first."

Warrior reached for his phone and used the speed dial.

"Mender," with a trembling tone in his voice, "Meet me at the church building in 5 minutes." He quickly hung up.

It must be serious, thought *Mender*, *I'd better hurry.*

CHAPTER 7

*""But the fruit of the Spirit is ... **Goodness** ... Galatians 5:22-23"*

"Look what Ben found." said *Warrior*, extending the book to *Mender*.

Mock Fenk Fist Legend was the title.

"Wait a minute. Is that the old book? Why does it have the same name as our town?" *Mender* continued at a rambling pace, "So, you are telling me there is a legend behind the name of our town, and there was a book written about it? This is extraordinary!" Quickening her pace, she continued, "I can wait to find out what all of this means. But wait, is this book really talking about our town? Because it has not been long ago that we changed the name, so there should not be a book with legends….about a newly named town. Don't you think there is something fishy here?" *Mender* finished, inquisitively.

"*That* is what we need to find out first," *Warrior* said with resolve.

"*Warrior*, look," *Mender* held out her hands, "I haven't been able to stop shaking since I laid my eyes on that book, and I don't know why."

"It is time to read it and find it out," *Warrior* declared.

They set to work, reading the book and cataloged everything of significance that they came across.

"Well, the book is filled entirely with images, and no text whatsoever," *Mender* murmured.

"Wait, what is this city? It's beautiful." She turned the book sideways to examine the picture. "What are all these battles? These people look familiar to me but it's too blurry. Oh look! There's text here, in the margin."

"Get the loop, let's see if we can read it."

Mock Fenk Fist, The Kingdom of Conquerors.

"What does it even mean? Kingdom, conqueror...I don't understand it, *Warrior*." *Mender* observed, "The city and the people from this book do not look anything like our town or people. I don't understand what is going on, the name looks the same, but these are not the same cities. I am confused."

"Me too, *Mender*, *Warrior* proclaimed, "Let us continue reading."

"Well, you mean looking at the images, because I've only seen that one phrase so far and I'm totally clueless," responded *Mender*.

"Look!" *Warrior* exclaimed, pointing to a section of the image, "It's just like my dream. I remember this. These two men here look like *Assassin* and *Poisson Dagger*. They look strong." He mused gravely, "They are fighting with everyone and it seems they win every time. This is giving me goosebumps..."

"What is this?" *Mender* gestured to the clash in the middle of the picture where the battle was concentrated.

"I don't know, but there is something hidden, they look like they are trying to destroy it. Also, It looks as if they're preventing these people from reaching it. Look," he said, "there's more text here.

They read it together aloud, "Secret Entrance."

"Apparently, *half* of the book is missing. Look here." *Warrior* pointed to a section of the spine that clearly showed many pages had been torn out.

"I am more confused now than before we picked the book up," said *Warrior*, and *Mender* nodded in agreement. "One thing is for certain, this book is not talking about our town." Setting the book down, he turned to *Mender*, "Did you notice that it is always referring to a kingdom? Our town is not, nor has it ever been a kingdom. The book never refers to a city or town, therefore, Mock Fenk Fist Kingdom is not our town."

"We have to pray and ask for guidance on this one," *Warrior* spoke decidedly, "I am starting to feel uneasy with this book. I'll ask Ben where he found it, and we can try to locate the other half. Let's agree to meet for prayer at 11am."

"Sounds good. See you then." *Mender* concluded.

Both heroes went about their chores for the remainder of the day, but their minds were filled with something indescribable.

The next day, when *Warrior* and *Mender* arrived at the building, they felt an overwhelming presence. The building resembled an old library, with lots of visible shelves, still housing some old, worn out books. Most were worthless.

"Ben's been sneaking out to this old abandoned building with some new friends, and on the last excursion, they found this book."

The two continued searching, but to no avail. They were ready to give up and leave, when *Mender* screamed.

"You have got to see this!"

"I'll be right there, hang on!" *Warrior* called down from the second story overlook.

"What, what is it?" *Warrior* exhaled, catching his breath. "I don't see any books." *Warrior* was a little annoyed.

"I know, right?" she said.

"So, what is it that I'm supposed to observe here? Because I don't get it," retorted *Warrior*.

"Look closer," *Mender* whispered, "And tell me you can see it."

"I still don't see anything," He spat.

Mender pointed her finger toward a small spot on a rotten wall.

"Look at that over there."

"It's an inscription, but what does it say?"

"Don't you get it? It is the same one that was on the final page of the book! But some letters are missing."

.nt.a.ce

"Just replace the dots with the missing letters and you will have the word *entrance*."

"You're right," *Warrior* spoke in amazement, "But I don't see the word *secret* anywhere."

"Well, there's a shape that looks like a hand next to it. Should we try it? Should I place my hand on it, *Warrior*?" she asked.

"Sure, but stop acting like a teenager, all excited so suddenly," he chided.

Beaming, *Mender* placed her hand on the wall over the mark. With a rumble and a crack, a large fissure appeared in the wall, and it looked like it was going to split the whole building in two. The fissure was large enough for someone to sneak in. Suddenly, out of nowhere, a *Mocking Man* sprung into existence, swinging his fist like lightning, hitting *Warrior* and *Mender* at the same time, and throwing them to the ground, disappearing instantly.

"What was that?" both groaned.

"It hurt, whatever it was. I feel like a truck just ran over me," said *Warrior* in a daze.

Just then, a booming, male voice came out of the dark.

"No one is allowed to pass this secret entrance without being called."

Once again, with greater ferocity, the *Mocking Man* sprang out of nowhere, going straight for *Warrior* and *Mender*.

Warrior was able to block the tremendous fist coming at him, but *Mender* was not so lucky.

"Flee, trespassers, or you will pay with your lives."

They could hear the warning, but were still unable to see the person speaking

"I am *The Guardian* of Mock Fenk Fist Kingdom, and you are not welcome. No human is allowed! Go from here!" With the last words, an immensely strong wind blew them out of the building, landing in the street..

"What has just happened?" thought *Warrior* and *Mender*.

"Man, I hurt," creaked *Mender*, "Did you see him?"

"No, I did not see him." *Warrior,* coughing up the words with blood as he stammered to his feet.

"I am intrigued and freaked out at the same time."

"*The Guardian* of Mock Fenk Fist Kingdom… No human is allowed…"

"*Mender,* we need to treat our injuries first then sit down, reflect and pray over this."

"Don't worry, I'm fine…it was nothing. But we definitely need to pray about it. We need to keep this to ourselves for now, and investigate further into this mystery. I am sure it has something to do with the old book Ben found. *That man's words are engraved in my mind.*"

"Wait," said *Mender,* "*The Guardian* said, *Without being called.* What do you suppose that meant?"

"Yes, I thought about that too. No human, kingdom…this is something curious. As *Shrewder* always says, *this is heavy.*"

Warrior, continued putting his thoughts in order, "He also mentioned a kingdom. Now, I am hundred percent sure this is about a hidden kingdom somewhere in this town. We need to solve this and I believe the answer lies with the one that just kicked our ass,"

CHAPTER 8

*"But the fruit of the Spirit ...**Faithfulness** ... Galatians 5:22-23"*

A few weeks passed by, and the team was not getting any answers from the Lord, and these thoughts continued pressing in their minds. They were praying, fasting and reading the Word of God together at church. One evening, out of nowhere, they heard in their hearts, *Your biggest challenge is coming, something you have never seen before. NEDE LAND.*

Warrior and *Mender* were troubled by this. There was no other instruction... *And what does NEDE LAND even mean?* they thought.

"You see, I told you there is a big mystery here. I bet this Nede Land has to do with *The Guardian.* This is getting seriously complicated. I think it is time to share our experience with the others," said *Mender.*

At this moment, *Warrior* and *Mender* decided to set up an e-meeting with their fellow team members. They needed to share what happened to them, as a warning, in case the others were going through similar situations.

All the teams were present for the e-meeting. *Warrior* and *Mender* filled them in about the current threat and situation. They all inquired about the meaning of *kingdom - no human - without being called*, but nobody had a clue, nor did anyone have any ideas about *Nede Land*. *Warrior* and *Mender* left out the part where they were beaten by a mysterious man. They did not want others to know that they were thrashed by some unknown individual, at least not yet.

"Has anyone ever heard about Nede Land?" All the team members were just listening and praying at the same time. Even with no ideas, they all felt that something was coming. *Something* was going to happen very soon and they must be ready.

The Emissary started by saying "There is something I have been thinking of sharing with you all, but the time had not yet arrived. In fact, I don't think you are ready to hear it, even now."

"Is it about Nede Land?" asked *Warrior*.

"Yes, it is." He paused before speaking again, "I am sure all of you have been having dreams that you cannot explain, and sensing something evil lurking in the shadows. We will have time to speak about all of this. But right now, we must prepare. *Warrior* and *Mender* heard *the biggest challenge* of our lives is coming. Allow me to pray a little bit more, and let us have another e-meeting 3 days from now. I advise all of you to dedicate time to praying and reading God's Word. It will help give a better understanding of this new situation. Have you all found the ancient books within your cities?"

They all replied with "Yes," excepting one team.

"Pray, because our threat is real and not of this kingdom," concluded *The Emissary*.

Three days later, the team was ready for their next meeting and eager to hear what *The Emissary* had been hiding, but now willing to share with them.

"Is everyone present?" asked Anthony, the team leader.

Everyone said, "Yes."

"Then, let us pray. Then I will hand over the lead of the meeting to *The Emissary*. He has something to share with all of us, something of the most importance for our next adventure. Let us pray then," said *Warrior*. After finishing the prayer, he handed over the meeting to *The Emissary*. "If you remember, when we were told to conquer these cities, it was for a very good reason. The cities where we are located and have won for the Lord, each one holds an ancient secret. They are strategic cities, stepping stones leading to a new world, one that is not of this earth. It is a spiritual world." said *The Emissary*.

The team members were listening carefully, intently, to *The Emissary*. He continued, staring into the eyes of the people on the screen.

"As *Warrior* and *Mender* have come to realize, in each city there is a secret entrance to a kingdom. As there are six cities, there are six respective kingdoms located in this new spiritual world known as, Nede Land. That is the importance of locating these ancient books. Within the books is the information we need to find the kingdom's entrances."

Then, *The Emissary*'s tone shifted, and he held up a finger in admonishment, saying,

"Do not take it lightly. There is a *Guardian* for each entrance and he will not allow you to pass, unless you are either called to that kingdom, or you defeat him." The tension increased as the team members shifted nervously in their seats.

"This is not like the other battles we have fought. It is completely different. We all need to fight the *Guardians*, and enter these new kingdoms. We will be tested, and we will need to learn what the Lord is trying to teach us through this challenge."

Warrior, interjecting, said, "But, *Emissary,* we did not feel any evil presence when *The Guardian* attacked us, and I must say this now, when he *thrashed* the floor with us."

"And you may never sense an evil presence," replied *The Emissary* with a wave of his hand.

"As I said before, we cannot say whether they are evil or not. The guardians simply defend their posts at all times, fighting like no other opponents we may have fought before. You must be victorious against *The Guardians.* Otherwise, I feel the worst will befall us."

The meeting was successful, and everyone went to their respective towns. "*Warrior,* it means that this new spiritual world of Nede Land must have something to do with the dark cloud affecting viciously upon the lives of the people on the outskirts town. We must go back to the entrance and get rid of whatever is creating these people's suffering in sickness and debauchery. We could be their only hope," added *Mender.*

• • • • • • • • •

"**M**ock Fenk Fist Kingdom," *Mender* puzzled, "I think it is time to face *The Guardian*." *Warrior*, standing beside her, agreed with a nod.

"We need to know what this is all about."

When *they* arrived at the location, *The Guardian* attacked them without hesitation, but this time they were able to *see* it.

"I said you are not welcome here! Retreat or be destroyed!" *The Guardian* shouted, as he swung, sweeping wildly at the team members.

"We'll see about that!" called *Mender*, leaping into action. "Leave this to me, *Warrior!* I want a chance to test him. I've been out of practice for a long time," She was dodging and ducking *The Guardian*'s attacks, "It's time for some exercise," she grinned.

"You're out of your mind, Woman. Do you think you can defeat me?" laughed *The Guardian*.

Summoning all her strength, *Mender* lunged at *The Guardian*. "I am your opponent now, show me what you got! I don't think you'll be able to defeat me with your bare fists."

"You will find out why *I* am *The Guardian* of Mock Fenk Fist, Woman." He attacked her with his full strength, breaking *Mender*'s sword as she tried to deflect the blow. But, before her sword hit the ground, an incredible light emerged and blinded *The Guardian*'s eyes for a second; then, he felt a sword touching his arm.

"Impressive," murmured *The Guardian*, "You were able to reach me with your sword. I became distracted for a moment. People who mock our Fenk Fist will become subject to the same. That is why I am *The Guardian* of Mock Fenk *Vanquish* Fist. I will vanquish anyone who dares to mock or challenge me."

He rose and rushed *Mender*, preparing his final blow.

"Not so fast, *Guardian.* I won't stand by and see my partner get hurt!" said *Warrior*, jumping into the fray, blocking the *Guardian*'s iron fist with his sword.

Seizing the opportunity, *Mender* cried out, *"Fusion!"*

Both *Warrior* and *Mender* were engulfed in light, and as it faded, they both stood holding swords, wreathed in otherworldly flames, flashing in all directions.

With these new powers, they were able to engage in a fierce battle that went on for more than 20 minutes.

One of *Warrior's* special attacks sent *The Guardian* to the ground.

"Nobody has ever been able to hurt me, or knock me to the ground. You two are formidable opponents. You have earned the right to pass. Be aware, what you have seen is nothing compared to what awaits you. You will hear the call when the door opens for you to enter the kingdom. Be vigilant and watch for the signs." With that, *The Guardian* disappeared.

CHAPTER 9

*"But the fruit of the Spirit is ...**Gentleness** ... Galatians 5:22-23"*

Nede Land is the first, and most wonderful world created for humankind to happily live in. Humans don't have much information about it, though. In fact, except for a short record contained in an ancient book, human's know nothing of its existence. The story says that the Creator's goal when creating Nede Land, was happiness; it was the first paradise on earth. Despite this, somewhere along the way, darkness crept into the paradise, enticing and deceiving humankind, appealing to their nature, causing their fall.

Because of human actions, Nede Land was hidden from sight, lost forever, or so everyone thought. A Guardian was placed at each entrance of its six Kingdoms, sealed by the Word of God. Its location has never been discovered, until now.

Many have tried to find it, but all have failed. As years passed by and civilization started to grow, the other kingdoms emerged, working as a shield for

Nede Land's secrets and treasures. Tales and ancient books were planted by God for seekers to find in case someday Nede Land called them.

Nede Land is a long lost and cast away world because of the terrible secrets dwelling within it. Secrets hidden from, and forbidden to, humankind. They are the most terrible and powerful secrets of all time.

Mock Fenk Fist Kingdom

The fourth head of the river Teseuphra, coming from Hont Well Kingdom, waters the land of this peaceful, quiet kingdom. History says other kingdoms used to exploit the hospitality and peacefulness of Mock Fenk Fist. They are not the fighting type, but they have mastered their *emotions*, learning to avoid fights at almost any cost. Meditation and the attainment of peaceful resolutions are most important to the citizens of this kingdom. People in this kingdom are hardworking and strictly adherent to their traditions and rules.

The story goes that a long time ago, other kingdoms tried to overtake them by force, sending hostile forces, disturbing their peace and abusing their hospitality. The people took a stand and started fighting back, maintaining their lifestyle and peace. The foreigners had underestimated this kingdom, but when the battle started, every single citizen in the kingdom fought like a warrior monk; women, children, men, even the elderly.

Among these warrior monks was a fearless fighter named *Kouken*. His fighting style was one of a kind, using his fists almost exclusively. He fought against the attacks on the kingdom, side by side with another warrior, the one they call *Narnish*. Rumour has it, *Narnish* was a bloody fighter, killing, stealing and deceiving everywhere he went. He was insatiable; there was no stopping him. He wanted to find the ultimate fight, believing it would grant him redemption for his crimes.

One day, while engaged in one of his sordid and ruinous campaigns, *Narnish* met three warriors and one of them was *Kouken*. *Narnish* fought with the other two warriors first, defeating them after only minutes. He thought it would be the same with *Kouken,* but the battle went on until exhaustion set in. There was no clear winner in the end, but neither were disappointed. Satisfied for the first time in their lives, they became friends, building their own town along with the other two fighters.

They combined their invincible fighting styles, creating the legendary Mock Fenk Fist style, and named their training house after it as well. The legend grew, people came to practice their incredible style, in hopes of finding peace. As time passed, the house became the kingdom we know today; Mock Fenk Fist Kingdom. The other two warriors died, leaving behind a great legacy in the kingdom, and giving life to their dynasties. The sons of these two warriors were able to learn new styles, and eventually merged them with those of their fathers. *Master Kouken* and *Headmaster Narnish* also created their own personal styles.

The kingdom enjoys fertile soil, perfect for harvesting and livestock to graze upon. They grow their own food and sell their supplies to the other kingdoms which are some of the best and freshest products in Nede Land; they are not interested in profit, because of their way of life. Taking great pride in their fighting heritage, citizens train hard every year earning the right to participate in Hont Well Kingdom's tournament.

Training is part of their daily lives. Starting at a very young age, they are enabled to develop incredible stamina and strength. Every year they advance to a new rank of training, each of which are superintended and administered by their own masters. Only when the students have reached maximum level, can they learn the secrets behind Mock Fenk Fist style. When they are ready, they demonstrate their skills and attempt to earn the right to learn the secret teachings of their techniques.

• • • • • • • • •

"No humans."

Mender was still speaking thoughtfully, "I still do not understand why *The Guardian* said no humans could enter the kingdoms, and yet, we received word from *The Elite Commander* to go to these kingdoms, claiming them for the Lord."

"Of course, I am human. So, how are we going to do this? A better question would be, how is it going to *happen?* Do we have to die? I am ready to die, if that's what it takes to claim these kingdoms." *Warrior* was sharing his thoughts and concerns with *Mender.*

"There are too many questions and, honestly, I don't have any answers," said *Mender.* "We just need to be ready, and continue praying to the Lord, for guidance and instructions."

Suddenly, a Bible verse popped into both their minds.

And the eyes of them both were opened.

"*Their eyes were opened*…are you thinking what I'm thinking *Mender?*"

And both of them said in unison, almost like an inspired speech,

"Our eyes will be opened to the spiritual world. We have been able to see the spiritual world around us, populated with demons and angels. But have we truly *seen* the spiritual world around us?"

Then alone, *Mender* spoke, "No, we have not."

Then another bible verse rushed into their minds and hearts.

I was in the Spirit on the Lord's day.

"Ok, now it makes more sense to me," *Mender* blurted with inspiration and self-discovery.

They shared the same spirit, and were having the same thoughts that *The Elite Commander* was instructing them through their minds and hearts. Their other teammates, in their respective cities were also receiving direct instructions on how to proceed with this new adventure.

It *is through the Spirit of the Lord that you will be able to see, your eyes will be opened to the spiritual realm and you will finally see.*

There was no need for a conference call or meeting of any kind among the teams; they were all listening to the instructions from their respective cities. Their thoughts were one. The message was as clear as the sun on a cloudless day.

We cannot walk into this new world in our human form; we need to walk in our spirit form. There are secrets you need to unveil in each kingdom. Your task is to conquer each kingdom, retrieving these secrets immediately. There are nine relics, powerful and fearsome. Secure them from these kingdoms and bring them back. You will need these relics to unlock your maximum potential and reveal the truth to the world. Beware, only by retrieving these relics will you be able to discover the two most terrible and powerful secrets of all time... hidden in Nede Land.

CHAPTER 10

*""But the fruit of the Spirit is ...**Self-control** ... Against such there is no law. Galatians 5:22-23"*

In one voice the team spoke these words, "We can see now, and hear the call. It is time to enter the kingdom."

Warrior and *Mender* knew it was their time to head to the entrance of the kingdom. They were unclear as to what challenges awaited them, but they were ready to face anything.

. . . .

I am awake, but I think I must be daydreaming, thought *Narnish, Headmaster* of Mock Fenk Fist Kingdom. He was puzzled as to why the loud alarm bell was ringing throughout the kingdom.

The monks and other inhabitants of the kingdom were astonished by the sound of the bell.

"No, that is not possible. There must be some mistake," the *Headmaster* said softly to himself. "That old bell has *never* rung before. For that bell to ring, my *Guardian* would have been defeated. No mortal could accomplish that," his disbelief was slowly becoming fear, "That is the bell from the human kingdom isn't it, *Kouken*?"

"*Headmaster*, I was too embarrassed to tell you about a little mishap I had with two interesting people..." *Kouken* shifted and coughed nervously, "Who *might* have earned the right to enter the kingdom."

"You must be trying to tease me, but instead you're testing my patience. We need to have a talk later about this," the *Headmaster* sternly spoke.

Through the loudspeaker system, the *Headmaster* announced,

"Attention all citizens of Mock Fenk Fist Kingdom. You are to continue with your daily routines and chores without interruption. If you see intruders, do not engage in battle. I repeat, *do not* engage. You are to immediately notify *Master Nampi* of Leitai Team. That is all."

· · · · · · · ·

Leitai Team is known as the cruelest team in all of Mock Fenk Fist Kingdom, and *Master Nampi* is the most brutal of all the *Masters*. They say that *Nampi* was a former champion fighter from an underground arena, and his skills were so ferocious, they forbade him from fighting in the underground altogether. In a search for redemption in Nede Land, he found *Headmaster Narnish*, who took him in and taught him to control and focus his skills.

Headmaster Narnish decided to make *Master Nampi* the leader of the Leitai Team, with a single purpose in mind; train the most deadly warriors in all of Nede Land, selecting the very best among them, to fight in Hont Well Kingdom's annual tournament.

• • • • • • • •

Every single one of *Master Nampi*'s students were looking for the opportunity to show their talents in real battle, and this was the *perfect* opportunity. The strongest ones, as brutal as their master, volunteered to take down the intruders.

"*Master Nampi*, these intruders must be strong, for they have defeated *Kouken*. Grant us the privilege of showing them retribution for their mistake! We will not let you down *Master!*" shouted *Koroshiya San*, with fiery pride. *Poisson Dagger* was listening, showing his eagerness to fight with light in his eyes.

"Very well," boomed *Master Nampi* in a commanding voice, "Koroshiya *San* and *Poisson Dagger* will take care of the intruders." He turned to the volunteers, 'Do not take this lightly by underestimating your opponents. After all, they defeated *Kouken*."

• • • • • • • •

"**W**hy should the *Leitai* team have all the fun?" grumbled some members of the Patrol Unit.

"We will keep patrolling and hope to bump into them. Then we will report that they attacked us first so we don't get into trouble with *Master Nampi* or *Headmaster Narnish*. Let's decide who is going to be the first to fight."

"Don't worry about it," said another member of the Patrol Unit., "Let us find them first before the Leitai Team does. Once *we* find them, we will test their strength. I do not think these weaklings can put up a good fight against us!"

"It's not like we are disobeying *Headmaster Narnish's* orders or something. We are just doing our regular patrol work!" and they all laughed.

. . . .

After entering through the entrance where they defeated *The Guardian, Warrior* and *Mender* found themselves by the shores of a glistening river. There was no one around, and they could see a trail leading to what looked like a town.

"Let us follow this trail carefully," said *Warrior,* shaking off the haze of the portal. "We still don't know what or who will come our way. I'm not sure if we entered this kingdom unnoticed, or if someone is already on the way."

"It is time to be mindful in our steps from here on," added *Mender.*

"Also, it is not a good idea to be walking around transformed like this. It would be better if we looked like regular people and not fighters," remarked *Warrior.*

"Yes, walking around like black-garnet knights is not the best plan," laughed *Mender.*

They walked for close to ten minutes without encountering anyone when, suddenly, *Mender* heard some voices in the distance. They were speaking and laughing loudly.

"*Warrior*, stop and listen. Someone is approaching."

"Yes, I can hear them. Let's get off the trail and hide in the forest until they pass," suggested *Warrior.*

"It looks like they are peasant monks or something. They're heading to the river. Phew! That was a close one," he said with relief in his voice, "We do not really want to hurt the citizens. Our task is to conquer and retrieve. If we can achieve our objective with few casualties, then all the better."

• • • • • • • • •

There was a big plantation by the river, where farmers go to cultivate the fields and fish daily. They never had to worry about intruders before, and they were not going to start now.

"*Headmaster Narnish* has appointed *Master Nampi's* team to locate and defeat the intruders," said one of the passersby.

They did not know that there was someone listening to their conversation.

"Did you hear what they were talking about?" asked *Warrior.*

"Yes, I did," responded *Mender*, "They mentioned something about some master named Ipman or nam-something or other. I am not sure. I could not catch it, but I know for sure they already know we are here. There is a group out there looking for us," she finished speaking in time to hear the others talking again.

"Guys!" whispered one of the fighters, "I see something moving behind those trees. Let us split up and surround the area. I think today is our lucky day! Let us hope it is them."

"What are you talking about?" asked another member of the Patrol Unit.

"Man! Sometimes you surprise me. The intruders, who else!? Why would we be this far from the kingdom if not to catch them?"

"Yeah! You're right."

• • • • • • • • •

Warrior and *Mender* allowed the patrol to capture them.

"Well, well, well! What do we have here?" asked one of the patrol guards, snidely.

"*Warrior,* I don't think we can escape this one, they've got us surrounde*d," played Mender.*

"You're not from around here, are ya? Why are you here and what do you want?" they inquired, "Answer us before we beat you senseless!" He continued tauntingly, "Look, guys! It's only a man and a woman, they don't represent any challenge to us."

Warrior, not having spoken yet, raised his eyes, looking directly at the men who were still mocking and laughing. In a calm voice he said,

"So, you are the unlucky ones." The guards stopped for a moment, but he continued, "I'll tell you what, since we want to avoid unnecessary casualties in our quest, why don't you point us in the direction of your leader's stronghold. We will let you leave unharmed.

Then *Mender* added, "Let us pass and no harm will come to any of you."

Upon hearing these words, the guards burst into a fit of laughter. Their laughs were different from before; they were more sinister and evil, tinged with sick contentment.

"Oh boy! You surely made our day. We were counting on finding you before anyone else did. We wanted to see how strong you are," one of the men boasted, "As a matter of fact, you might call us *eager*. As you can see, there is only one way for you to get away alive." As he finished his sentence, they all drew their swords.

"Well, you asked for it. We wanted you to go unharmed, but it seems like there is no other way," said *Mender*, "*Warrior*, may I have the honors?"

"Be my guest," answered *Warrior*.

"All five of you can participate. Don't worry, I won't bite you," said *Mender*, cheekily. *Warrior* proceeded to sit himself on ground, crossing his arms and legs while saying to the guards,

"It is *ladies first* after all. She's all yours."

"Your power must be colossal, Woman. You think you can take all five of us at once? Fine, I will go first," said one of the guards, haughtily.

When he went for her, *Mender* gave him one single blow, and he was down on the ground.

"I told you, all five…erh uh, *four* of you, sorry. All FOUR of you can attack at once," she laughed.

They were pissed, and decided to attack her all together. What they saw in that first rush was a flurry of impossibly strong fists, knocking them to the ground. Mender then used one of her most powerful techniques, which gave her the ability to perceive their attacks as if they were moving in slow-motion. In what seemed like an instant, the guards were writhing on the ground in pain, completely disoriented.

"You are strong, Woman, I give you that," wheezed one of the fighters on the ground.

"Follow our tracks in the mud and you will find our *Master.*" He then evaporated into a cloud of smoke.

CHAPTER 11

*"Now concerning **Spiritual Gifts**, brethren, I would not have you ignorant... 1 Corinthians 12:1-11"*

"When did you get that strong, *Mender*?" asked *Warrior*, "You did not even transform. I am impressed."

"Stop teasing me, *Warrior.*" His compliment made her smile.

They continued on their way, following the footsteps to reach the kingdom. But they did not realize that one of the guards was still alive.

The guard ran fast through the forest, returning to his *Master*, and giving him the bad news. When he reached *Master Musashi*'s post, he gave him all the details needed to assess the situation.

"You were told to not to engage the intruders. Your orders were to report to me, so I can report to *Master Nampi.*" The guard, stuttering, said,

"We bumped into them and they attacked us first."

"You mean, they *beat* most of you to death, you moron." *Master Musashi* was infuriated.

· · · · · · · · ·

"*Koroshiya San, Poisson Dagger*, move out! Search the area. Locate and finish them off! I have reports that the intruders have defeated members of the Patrol Unit. I don't want to report any more casualties to *Headmaster Narnish*. They are not even supposed to be here, much less defeat our fighters!"

"*Headmaster Narnish*, we have news about the intruders. They bumped into a Patrol Unit of five, attacked and defeated them. Only one of them was able to make it out alive and he is severely wounded.

"I see! The rumor is true. They *are* strong. I am not sure how they managed to defeat *Kouken*, but it seems we will find out very soon. I am sure they are coming for something more than a fight. They must have come for the *secret relics*," said *Headmaster Narnish*.

Once again, through the communication system, he said,

"Attention to all *Masters* and their units. The intruders were last seen near the river, crossing the forest towards the kingdom. You are free to engage the intruders. Take special precautions, they are dangerously strong. Show them who we are and bring me their heads!"

· · · · · · · · ·

The Patrol Unit was one of a kind, specializing in military strategy and combat. The reputation of their *Master* was known, not only in Mock Fenk Fist Kingdom, but also through most of Nede Land. Legend says that he was a Japanese general in ancient times of war.

He led one of the smallest armies his country could supply into a battle with an enemy over 20 times his number. Everybody thought he was crazy, that he was just looking for a glorious death in battle. They all told him that it was best to commit Hara Kiri. It would be more honorable for him than pursuing his and the entire regiment's death. The only words he spoke in reply were,

"I don't plan on dying, not just yet. This battle is mine."

When the rival general saw these few men forming a battle array to face his mighty army, he thought it was a joke and an insult to his honor.

"I will dash this arrogant bastard to pieces with only my horsemen. There is no need to waste arrows on this lunatic."

He sent the infantry, which was almost double the size of *General Musashi's* regiment.

It will all end in less than ten minutes. Thought the opposing general. And he was completely right. Five minutes later, all his horsemen were dead on the battlefield.

"How is this possible! How can this be!" the rival general shouted with anger. He was so blinded with fury that he did not see through *General Musashi's* ploy, and decided to lead the battle against this infuriating general *himself.* He mustered all his remaining forces and led them into the battlefield. But what they found was not defeat, no, what they found was *annihilation.*

No one knows exactly how the general won the battle, there are many rumors and speculations. Some say he had each one of his warriors dig big trenches in the battlefield with lances. Others say that his warriors were possessed by demons, able to kill off their enemies in a blink of an eye. Another theory is that *General Musashi* used some sort of dark power to defeat them. In the end, these are only rumors and nobody knows the truth, but *General Musashi* and his men.

After the incredible battle, the King at that time wanted *General Musashi* to train his entire army. The general refused the King's request, and as a consequence, the King demoted him to a mere foot soldier, dispersing all of his men into other battalions. The King was hoping *General Musashi* would reconsider his request, but instead, he vanished, never to be seen again. What no one knows is that one day the general stumbled upon *Headmaster Narnish*. He decided to abandon the way of the bushido and become a monk at Mock Fenk Fist Kingdom. After many years of meditation, *Headmaster Narnish* renamed him *Master Musashi*, and put him in charge of training the Patrol Units.

• • • • • • • •

"You are telling me that five members of the Patrol Unit were defeated and only one of them is alive?" asked *Master Musashi* in indignation.

"There's a new order for all the members of the Patrol Units! Find the intruders but do not fight them. You will lead them directly to me. I will take care of them personally."

Because of this order, all the members of the Patrol Unit felt invigorated. Excitement and high emotions ran through their minds.

"We will finally see our *Master* in a real fight."

Each guard in the Patrol Unit was searching for the intruders to deliver them to their master. Each one wanted to be the one to catch them. They could not allow the Leitai unit to find them first.

"We cannot let this shame rest on the Patrol Unit. Our master will avenge our comrades and return our honor!"

Warrior noticed that someone had been following their trail for some time, and whoever it was, he did not want to confront them. He'd been stopping whenever they stopped, and continuing whenever they continued.

"Have you noticed?" asked *Warrior*.

"Do you mean the person who has been following us for the past hour?" answer *Mender*, "Yeah, I've noticed."

"I think it is about time we find out who that person is and what he wants. Don't you think *Mender*?"

"Sure, let's pick up the pace, hide, and see if he tries to catch up with us."

"It sounds like a great idea." They burst into a sprint, and after about a hundred yards, they split, one to each side of the trail, and hid.

A few seconds later, a middle-aged man came running up the trail, looking in every direction. *Warrior* and *Mender* jumped out of their hiding places and subdued the man.

"Why are you following us?" demanded *Mender*, "Answer, before it's too late!"

"Please! Lower your voices!" pleaded the man. "They might hear you. I am not your enemy. I am here to help you." said the mysterious person.

"Help us? Explain yourself, and be clear," cautioned *Warrior*.

"Of course, of course," said the man with a trembling voice, "Allow me to introduce myself. My name is Gaido, and I was one of the most trusted advisors to *The Headmaster*. When I found out about an ancient prophecy and shared it with the people, *The Headmaster* became infuriated with me. He even demoted me to a mere servant in the outskirts of the Kingdom. Do you know what it is like to be on top of the world one day, only to have everything taken away from you the next?" spat Gaido with an angry and resentful voice, "Of course, you don't, how could you? They threw me into the street like a dog."

CHAPTER 12

*"To another **Wisdom** by the same Spirit. 1 Corinthians 12:8-11"*

"**We** understand your words. But I'm curious, what was this prophecy that brought you so low?" asked *Warrior.*

"Oh! You two are so naïve! You don't know what you got yourself into, do you? *The Headmaster* is like the King of Mock Fenk Fist Kingdom. He is the most powerful and cruel fighter of them all. Of course, he left that life behind a long time ago, but I know his true nature." The man looked to *Mender,* then to *Warrior* slyly, as if signifying he had some hidden knowledge.

"Not only are the other masters around him just as cruel, or even crueler, they are viciously loyal. The five fighters you defeated were part of an elite Patrol Unit, and their leader is *Musashi.* He was a samurai and a general before joining the kingdom. They say there was no one like him in battle, and that his swordsmanship was unparalleled. You guys made a big mistake by crossing him," he said with an edgy laugh.

"Not only that," continued Gaido, "The unit in charge of finding, and kicking you out of the kingdom, is none other than the Leitai Team. Their master is one called *Nampi*. If you thought *Master Musashi* was intense, *Master Nampi*'s stronger and scarier than he is. They say that after *The Headmaster, Master Nampi* is the strongest in the kingdom."

Warrior and *Mender* had been listening very carefully to this story, assessing the situation being described to them. For the first time, they were receiving intel on their target, and they planned to get as much information as possible from Gaido.

"And what about the prophecy you mentioned before?" pressed *Mender*.

"Ah, well, there is a prophecy in Mock Fenk Fist. People think that it is just a myth, not to be taken seriously. Most even think there is just one prophecy, but I have studied them all, and I can attest that the first one came true. I saw it with my own eyes!"

"My friend, what does the prophecy say?" *Mender* insisted.

"The prophecy goes like this...

A nameless descendant of Mock Fenk Fist will fight against the other kingdoms in Nede Land. He will

bring chaos, and destruction. He will destroy the
world as we know it, and in its place build a new one.
It will be a world of peace and happiness.

"The same prophecy mentions two warriors that
come from a faraway land. These two will fight the
strongest combatants in the Mock Fenk Fist Kingdom
and they will win; thus retrieving the secret treasures.
However, they will fail to unify all the kingdoms of
Nede Land, and will face great deception."

"That is too much information for me to understand
at the moment," said *Warrior*, clearly overwhelmed.

"It is ok, you don't need to understand it," the man
grinned, "You are *part* of this prophecy." *Warrior* and
Mender were taken aback.

"Still, you don't see it. But I do. You will set the stage
for the one that needs to come. You must be careful
because you may face deception on your quest,"
warned Gaido.

"So, why do you want to help us?" asked *Mender*,
searching for a hold on the moment.

"I thought it was obvious from my story. I believe in
the prophecies, and I know that you are part of them.
I will help you fulfil as much of them as I can."

"Is it not because you resent your *Headmaster*?" asked *Warrior*.

"No, it is not. But, I will get some satisfaction from seeing him destroyed." The man clenched his fist as he spoke with glee.

"How do we know that you are not going to rat us out?" *Mender* asked suspiciously.

"You don't. But do you see anyone else around here offering to help you with your quest? *The Headmaster* has called for your heads to be brought to him on a silver platter. But I have good news for you, my friends; I am one of the few who knows the secret passages of the kingdom. I can take you through the kingdom faster and safer, with fewer casualties to my fellow men. But..."

"I knew it, there is always a "but"," said Warrior, "What's the problem?"

"Well, the fastest way leads us directly to *The Master* of the Patrol Unit."

"You mean to that *Musashi* guy, don't you?" asked *Mender*.

"Exactly. There is a longer path, but it would take months to navigate undetected."

"Take us through the shortest one," said *Warrior*.

"I feared you would say that," continued Gaido. "Be prepared for anything with *Master Musashi*, or it might be the end of your journey."

Warrior confidently reassured him, "Do not worry about it. We will handle him."

• • • • • • • • • • •

After only 15 minutes of walking through secret tunnels, they reached the secret entrance leading into the Kingdom. They were only mere steps away from the Patrol Unit station.

"We are here. Once I open this little hatch, you are on your way. Are you sure you want to do this?" asked Gaido with a tense tone in his voice.

"Yes, we are. We will be fine Giado. Thank you very much for your assistance," whispered *Mender*.

"You are most welcome. One last thing," said Gaido, "You know that if by some miracle you defeat *Master Masashi*, you will be taken prisoner immediately. If you don't go willingly, be ready to fight over 20 trained soldiers from the patron unit."

"We understand, and we are ready for the outcome of this battle," said *Warrior*.

"Can I give you a piece of advice?" Gaido said, insistently.

"Sure, go ahead," confirmed *Mender*.

"If you manage to defeat the master of the Patrol Unit, do not resist. Let them take you to *The Headmaster*. This will be the easiest way for you to find what you are looking for. Of course, I don't advise you to fight *Headmaster Narnish*. Instead, you can request an honorable duel with one of his best warriors. If you defeat *Headmaster Narnish*'s fighter, he will be honor bound to bestow anything you want. Don't be foolish, trying to be heroes. Heroes do not fair well in this kingdom."

"Gaido," murmured *Warrior*, in a contemplative tone, "Open the hatch, we are ready." *Warrior* placed his hand on the man's arm, gratefully. "We really appreciate your concern, but we are on a quest and cannot stop under any circumstances."

"Understood. Here you go."

• • • • • • • • • • • •

"Farmers and servants created the secret tunnels hundreds of years ago. They were meant for the children to use. While training or working in the fields, children could use the tunnels to reach home quickly, getting supplies for their elders or trainers. *Mender* and Warrior cautiously left the protection of the tunnel, quickly coming upon the foe they sawt.

"After some time, the tunnel's existence was not known to many. Somehow, I was hoping you would make it to me without being caught," *Master Musashi* spoke in a calm sternly fashion, "I suspect someone helped you find this entrance, but that person is of no worry to me. I am just glad that you came." *Master Musashi* waved his hand in feigned graciousness. *Warrior* and *Mender* observed over 20 heavily armed guards kneeling to welcome them.

"I vowed to myself a long time ago that I would never kill again. That I would never rob a warrior of his life. But for you two, I will break that vow."

Warrior interrupted him, "Thank you for your kind words, *Master*, but we are on a quest and we have a goal to achieve. So, could we speed this up? I'll fight you myself, if you stop talking."

CHAPTER 13

*To another **Knowledge**. 1 Corinthians 12: 8-11"*

"I admire your courage and audacity, Boy. You make me feel rejuvenated with your taunting words. For your courage and bravery, I shall duel with you alone, sparing your companion. Of course, she will not remain free and will be taken to *The Headmaster.*"

"That's if *you* defeat *me*," said *Warrior*," But what will happen when *I* defeat *you*?" he asked.

"Hilarious! Let us pretend it is a possibility. All my men have strict orders to deliver you to *Headmaster Narnish*, who would then decide your fate. But, no need to worry about that eventuality, since you are about to draw your final breath," sneered *Musashi*.

"*Warrior*, be careful. He looks strong," warned *Mender*, But, I will beat the crap out of you if you dare to lose to him."

Warrior just winked at her. Meanwhile, the soldiers circled around the three of them, setting the stage for the impending fight. The whole unit shouted in one voice, "Ready!"

"You should take this fight more seriously," said *Musashi*. "Hmmm, I think those rags suit you."

No sooner than the taunt left his lips, *Warrior's* clothes transformed into a black suit of armor, surmounted with a golden helmet. In his left hand, a diamond shield appeared, along with a silver belt of perfect samite at his waist. Lastly, from the black plates of the armor, emerged a thousand glittering gemstones. As he moved, they seemed to ripple with all the colors of the rainbow, or like the fiery stars of heaven itself. Fear took hold of *Musashi* for the first time in his life, upon seeing this display of splendor.

What no one knew about *Musashi*, was that over the years, he had been having dreams about an incredible fight with a black knight, who was able to defeat his *Niten Ichi Ryu* style. He spent many years travelling all over the kingdom, learning different techniques and fighting styles. At the end, he created his own fighting style, called *Niten Ichi Ryu*, which meant *the strategy of two heavens as one or two swords as one*. It is invincible, or so he thought. Since no one in the

Kingdom has been able to defeat him, he had never considered the dream coming to fruition either.

"This cannot be real. It was just a dream," he reassured himself. But *Master Musashi* remembered that the warrior from his dream was wreathed in flames, and though he could not see any fire surrounding *Warrior*, he knew he had fire *in* him. *He cannot defeat me*, thought *Master Musashi* again.

A powerful fight took place, and the guards encompassing them were having trouble keeping up with the speed of the mighty attacks. *Master Musashi* had just switched a two-sword technique, enabling him to cut *Warrior* deeply, sending him to the ground. The wound was indeed grievous, and began to affect *Warrior*'s vision. *I have to do something or I might end up losing this battle*, thought *Warrior* to himself. In that split second thought, he felt another cut burn across his back.

Master Musashi said, "It is time to end this fight, Boy. Enjoy your last breath."

Just then, something changed about *Warrior*, as if that last slash awakened something in him. The *number 1* appeared on his upper right chest, showing his strength, though *Master Musashi* did not understand the meaning behind the number.

What is going on? He should be weakening, wondered *Master Musashi.*

Warrior leapt at *Musashi*, slashing and cutting with increased ferocity.

"Where is this power coming from?" yelled *Musashi* to *Warrior.*

"Do not worry about my power. All you need to know is that I'm not ready to die yet," asserted *Warrior.* His black Spartan sandals began emitting fire while he was moving, the fire increasing with the intensity of his attacks. The fire became so intense, it began to ignite the ground.

Warrior saw a moment of hesitation in *Master Musashi* and was able to land his first blow.

"Not so fast," shouted *Master Musashi*, "This is your end, not mine!" He used the last of his remaining strength to summon an incredible blur of attacks. *Musashi* thought this would surely end the fight, but the fire emanating from *Warrior's* black Spartan sandals blinded *Master Musashi.* As his sight recovered, he looked down to see *Warrior's* blade buried in his chest. The fight was over.

Musashi staggered backward, "I lost today because I did not know you," he struggled to speak, "I trusted my swords, but I underestimated my opponent." And with that, he let go of his final breath.

Although the soldiers were unnerved with the outcome of the fight, they needed to obey their *Master*'s final command.

"Move in!" As they pushed *Warrior* and *Mender*, *Warrior* began reaching for his sword.

"Easy *Warrior*," whispered *Mender*, "Remember our goal. Keep your calm."

• • • • • • • • • • •

Word got around quickly about the sudden, unexpected defeat of *Master Musashi*. The people were consternated, wanting to find and kill the intruders. After all, it was a long walk from the Patrol Unit to *Headmaster*'s temple.

All the members of the Patrol Unit were escorting *Warrior* and *Mender*. A multitude of angry peasants were gathering as part of their escort as well. They started yelling, "Kill them! Beat them!" Things were getting out of control when two individuals showed up in the middle of the street, blocking the procession.

The Patrol Unit had to stop, because they would not move.

"We have orders to take the prisoners to Headmaster Narnish!" the commander shouted, "Step aside if you don't want to die!"

When *Warrior* and *Mender* saw the two opposing men, they could not believe their eyes.

"Am I dreaming?" asked *Mender* to *Warrior*, "Is that *Assassin* and *Poison Dagger*?"

"I'm afraid so," said *Warrior*, grimly.

"But we defeated *Assassin* and *Poison Dagger* already. How on earth are they here?" puzzled *Mender*.

"I don't know but I don't like what I'm feeling. This is becoming a nightmare."

Eventually, the guards and the crowd stepped aside, since they were afraid of the Leitai Team, especially the one they called *Koroshiya San* and his partner *Poisson Dagger*.

Without a word the aggressors bolted, swords drawn, with all their strength, towards *Warrior* and *Mender*. They wanted to kill them immediately; they did not want to turn them in. The glory was in the kill. *Warrior* was injured from his fight with *Musashi,* and when he tried to deflect a blow from *Poisson Dagger*, he was knocked unconscious.

"I guess this one is already done. I cannot believe he defeated *Master Musashi*. What a disgrace!" gloated *Koroshiya San.*

"Me neither. They don't have what it takes to defeat us, but we will not show them mercy of any kind."

"Not so fast," said *Mender*, blocking their second wave of attacks.

"Woman, you are no match for us," snickered *Poisson Dagger*. Then *Mender* shouted defiantly, "We have defeated you once, we will defeat you again!"

"You are confused, Woman; you defeated the human shells we were using, not *us*. You are now in *our* kingdom. Your life ends today!"

Warrior was slowly waking up and he felt an overwhelming sensation of deja-vu when he opened his eyes. His dream was becoming a reality. He saw *Mender* on the ground, with *Assassin,* or Koroshiya San as he is known as in this world, stomping his foot on her throat while *Poisson Dagger* poised for the final blow.

"Time to die, Woman!" hissed *Poisson Dagger*. Then, *Mender* screamed, "Fusion!"

There was a crack of thunder and a flash of lightning splitting the sky. *Mender* transformed into a completely different warrior, as she catapulted back onto her feet. She was now a black knight in her full splendor with a glowing *number 8* on her breastplate. Standing beside her was a fully transformed *Warrior*. These numbers indicated the strength of the fighter. Their most lethal weapons were forged by the combining of their original ones. Each black knight was holding a large, devilishly sharp English Rapier that was flashing with brilliant light.

CHAPTER 14

*"To another the **Faith**. 1 Corinthians 12: 8-11"*

"How did she get away from us?" wondered both enemies. Fresh memories of the past started creeping into the minds of *Assassin* and *Poison Dagger.*

"This is not going to happen again. In our world, we are more powerful than ten of you put together. You cannot win this battle! You *will not* defeat us!" *Poisson Dagger* screamed.

Suddenly, the two black knights raised their left hands, and instantaneously became a blur of air and light, surrounding their foes. *Assassin* and *Poison Dagger* stabbed feebly into the whirling blur around them without any ill effect.

A spire of flames came out of the tornado, encapsulating the two enemies while the fiery sandals of *Warrior* and *Mender* blinded them. Unable to see, *Assassin* and *Poison Dagger* were now fighting without one of their strongest senses as they shouted,

"Blinding us won't be enough, *Cowards!* You will not defeat us!" They managed to hit *Mender* with a wild swing, and she started bleeding. *Assassin* used his fatal technique, *Honjo Masamune Dark Tornado,* which increased the speed of his attacks exponentially. With this speed he was able to deal a critical blow to both Mender and Warrior.

"We will reveal our real names to you before you die!" shouted *Assassin*, "I am *Mastema.*"

"And I am *Ipos!*" exclaimed *Poison Dagger.* The two demons they defeated in the past were now giving them the fight of their lives.

"You may have kicked us out of your world, but now the tables have turned and you are in ours," said the demon *Mastema*, presenting himself in full form.

"It is time to send them to the point of no return!" said the demon *Ipos,* now completely transparent.

When *Warrior* saw that *Ipos* was bleeding, he eagerly spoke, "It is time to end this! You ran away from our world, but you can run no longer! We came prepared for you. I now understand why we needed to come to the Mock Fenk Fist Kingdom in Nede Land. It was to finish you cowards off for good."

When *Mastema* and *Ipos* heard these words, they became so enraged their powers increased to that of a dark tornado, hoping it would engulf the righteous duo, and kill them. Too distracted by possible victory, the demons did not see the great light emitting from *Warrior* and *Mender.* This light, this holy fire, enveloped the demon. As they were consumed, the force of the wind generated by the fire pushed the crowd away from the road.

Kouken and Gaido came out of the crowd, taking advantage of the situation and commotion. They were able to drag *Warrior* and *Mender* away from the crowd and guards. The Kingdom's intruders had seemingly disappeared.

They had retreated to a small hovel which was inconspicuous and out of the way. *Kouken* kept it as a secret hiding place for just such an occasion.

"*Kouken?* Why are you helping us?" asked *Warrior,* "We knew about Gaido, but we never would have imagined you helping us."

"Silly of you. Who do you think *sent* Gaido to assist you the first time? Gaido is my trusted companion. We both follow the prophecies and know the secrets behind all of this."

Warrior and *Mender* were severely injured from their recent fight. It was a miracle they had help in this new kingdom, and from the most unexpected source.

"I think we need medical assistance. Is there anyone in the kingdom that wouldn't double-cross us?" asked *Mender.*

"I may have the perfect solution, but it will require two days," explained *Kouken*, "You see, once a year when the moon sets on top of the mountain, a fountain, at the head of the river, emanates healing waters. Our river, Teseuphra, has that special power. You see, *Headmaster Narnish* thinks he is the only one in the Kingdom who knows this secret and he will surely be there when the timing is right," explained *Kouken*.

"How come you know so much about it, *Kouken*?"

"I am *Kouken*, and if there is something hidden in this kingdom, I know about it."

"You mean, *we* know about it," said Gaido. "*Master Narnish* thinks that a magical spirit touches the waters of Teseuphra river, thus bringing healing power to that little fountain. Of course, he is not sure. No one knows for sure."

"In the meantime, you should rest and stay hidden. We need to devise a good plan to get you out of here unnoticed, and up to the foot of the mountain. Not only that, we need to make sure to avoid an encounter with *Headmaster Narnish* on this journey," *Kouken* said. Gaido, went on to say to the group,

"He is the only one who can open the entrance to the healing fountain. We need to get there before *The*

Headmaster arrives, and hide in the mountain. When he opens the entrance and goes inside, you will immediately sneak in after him. This is a very dangerous game we are playing. *Headmaster Narnish* is no one to be trifled with." Gaido stroked his chin contemplatively before relaying another concern.

"I just don't know how we will get out of there after *Headmaster Narnish* seals the entrance."

"Leave that to me," said *Kouken*, "I once followed *Headmaster Narnish* up the mountain and through the entrance without being detected. I was able to get in, but I could not get out. After being trapped for days, almost giving up and nearly dying from thirst, I discovered a way to get myself out."

"Excellent!" clapped Gaido, "We have a good and crazy plan for after tomorrow."

"Now, let us get to the most important part of your journey," said *Kouken.*

"Well, *Warrior*'s not going anywhere because of his injuries, but I am sure you can get out of here and do a little reconnaissance for us. Am I wrong, *Mender*?" asked Gaido.

"That will be fun," said *Mender*, "My injuries were not as bad as Warrior's.

"I don't think it is wise for her to go out. The whole plan would be in jeopardy should someone recognize her," remarked *Kouken* in a concerned tone.

"There is no need to worry, I have it covered," said Gaido. He stepped closer to *Mender* with a sharp, inquisitive look on his face.

"We just need to get rid of this, this, and this. Change this…here, put this on…and voila! You look like one of us now." He had removed some of her accoutrements, replacing them with a few sundries from around the room, and gave her a cloak and hat native to the surrounding area.

"Impressive!" *Warrior* wheezed, trying to be positive, despite his injuries, "I can barely recognize you, *Mender.*"

"If anyone asks, we will say that you are my distant cousin who is visiting for a few days. Also, pretend that you are mute, otherwise, your accent will betray you!" They all laughed.

CHAPTER 15

*"To another **Gifts of Healings.** 1 Corinthians 12:8-11"*

Early the next morning, Gaido took *Mender* for a stroll in town.

The first thing *Mender* was struck by were the children working in the town, taking shifts out in the fields or in their respective shops, and fighting one another in makeshift rings and small dojos. They would work a few hours at their trade, then run to spar or fight directly afterward.

"This is very interesting," whispered *Mender*, "Women and children are practicing the art of fighting here. What kind of martial arts are they practicing?"

"Before they learn to master the secrets of Mock Fenk Fist, they train in all sorts of styles, wieling all kinds of weapons. They train their bodies to endure incredible strain as well. It takes them years to master these basics, and there is a different master for each fighting style. Each student must adapt to a myriad of expectations and teachings," said Gaido.

"They need to dedicate at least one full year with each master. Look…" Gaido gestured to a group of highly organized children of different ages. "This is the Karate group. Those over there are learning Jujitsu, and way over there are Aikido lessons. This group is for Judo *and* Hapkido, and we also have Kung Fu and Tai Chi." *Mender* could hardly keep up.

"As you can see, they need to train for six years in total before learning Mock Fenk Fist. In each one of these groups, they integrate one basic tenet of Mock Fenk Fist. When they master the ultimate art, they decide among themselves who will remain and teach, and who will be assigned as one of the kingdom's guards.

"Fascinating," wondered *Mender.*

"This is the farmer's side of the kingdom, where all our food is cultivated. As you can see, almost all of them are women. Most of the women seem to have a propensity for farming, but young boys spend time farming as well as the occasional man."

As they walked along, Gaido explaining and waving his hand around at all the interesting diversity in the town, Mender listened intently. They came upon a bustling square in which all manner of goods were being traded. Spices, vegetables, cloth and every other thing the kingdom had to offer.

"This is the market, where we display most of our products."

"Very peaceful kingdom, very beautiful…" commented *Mender,* her mouth open in amazement.

"Remember, you are mute. I wasn't kidding about your accent. Just listen and you will understand why."

"Sorry, my bad," *Mender* apologized.

Gaido and Mender strolled along the kingdom without any hassle. Eventually, they entered the temple and she was able to see *Master Nampi* and *Headmaster Narnish* from a distance. They did not want to get too close.

Such a strong kingdom, she thought.

"Remember, we are the kingdom of conquerors and are proud of it. Everyone in this kingdom knows how to fight, but we will always obey The Headmaster's orders."

• • • • • • • •

"What did you learn of the kingdom?" asked *Warrior,* struggling to sit up in his bed.

"I saw how strong and dedicated they are to perfecting their fighting skills," I also saw *Master Nampi* and *Headmaster Narnish*. They are fearsome, even from a distance. I sensed incredible power coming out of them."

Noticing *Warrior*'s wounds, she continued, "We need to get you to the healing waters soon. I'll be glad when we both can taste those magical waters."

· · · · · · · · ·

"The night is almost upon us, we need to get going," said *Kouken,* "Gaido, can you work your magic on *Warrior*? We don't want people to recognize him either."

"Certainly, but this will be more difficult." Gaido was indeed able to transform *Warrior*'s appearance, making him unrecognizable.

"Even more impressive. You have outdone yourself this time," complimented *Kouken.*

"Thank you very much, *Master.*"

"How many times have I told you not to call me that?"

"My apologies, it just slipped out."

"Wait a minute! *You* are one of the Masters in this kingdom? Why didn't you say that before?" shouted *Mender.*

"It would not change anything. Besides, I left the way of the Masters behind a long time ago. I became the humbled *Kouken.*"

He continued, "Indeed I was one of the most powerful Masters in the kingdom. Only *Headmaster Narnish* was capable of challenging me. I trained the best fighters in the kingdom." *Kouken* breathed deeply and raised his glance to meet *Warrior*'s. "But that was long ago. I chose another path. To become *Kouken, The Guardian* of the kingdom. But, that is enough about my past."

"It is time, Ladies," joked a giggling Gaido.

"I cannot believe that you dressed me as a woman. Not in a million years would I have wanted to see myself like this!" snapped *Warrior.*

"Don't worry, Sister! You look beautiful!" reassured Gaido, mockingly, "You are my sister and *Mender* is my cousin, should anyone ask. There should not be anyone on the road we are traveling, but just in case."

• • • • • • • • • •

The road to the Fountain of Healing Waters was a difficult one. Unfortunately, the group encountered several people on the way out of the kingdom which they had to evade.

"This is going well," sarcastically remarked Gaido to the group.

Suddenly, before crossing the border of the *kingdom's* capital, there came a voice from behind.

"*Kouken*, have you heard everything that has happened with the intruders?"

Turning to the man, astonishment took over as they realized who was speaking.

"Don't make a sound," whispered Gaido to *Warrior* and *Mender.*

"*Master Nampi*, how are you doing?" *Kouken* replied, in a friendly tone.

"I asked if you heard the stories about the intruders," rumbled the man in an aggravated tone. He was clearly not in a mood to tolerate pleasantries. He continued, moving closer with one enormous stride.

"I know someone inside the kingdom has been helping them. They could not have vanished without a trace by themselves. I will find them and when I do, they will regret having come to this kingdom," *Master Nampi* said, in a subdued manner. Underlying was a threatening, low growl of a wolf, warning off an unwelcome guest.

"Yes, I've heard. They are extraordinarily powerful. Indeed, you need to be careful *Master Nampi*. There is more to them than meets the eye," replied *Kouken*.

"Old man, you are getting soft and weak, and allowed yourself to be defeated by these two parasites. I have to see them for myself," retorted *Master Nampi*, carelessly.

Kouken laughed and said, "Yes, I must be getting too old for this." With that, the convoy continued on their way without further incident.

CHAPTER 16

*"To another **Working of Miracles**. 1 Corinthians 12: 8-11"*

Our disguised warriors hid themselves at the foot of the mountain, where none could see them.

"Don't even breath. *Headmaster Narnish* is coming," whispered *Kouken,* almost imperceptibly. *Warrior* was pondering the force he felt from *Master Nampi,* and how powerful the pressure had been. But when he felt *Narnish*'s presence, even from a distance, he was speechless.

"How powerful is this old man?" commented *Warrior.*

"Believe me, you don't want to know, and you definitely don't want to fight him. Now shut up, and be still," admonished *Kouken* "This is a fight you two must avoid at all costs. For your own sake."

"I'm beginning to believe you," said *Warrior.*

Headmaster Narnish mumbled some words they could not hear as he passed, and then proceeded to vanish.

"Where did he go?" *Mender* asked.

"He went into the cave where the fountain is hidden. Let us move in now. No sound or noise, or we are all done for," said *Kouken*.

As they moved, *Kouken* had to be quick, constantly redirecting them to the proper places.

"Where are you going, Gaido? That's a terrible spot to hide. Follow me." They crept slowly, with no sound at all, until they arrived at the next hiding spot.

"Now what?" *Warrior* questioned.

"All we can do now is wait until *Headmaster Narnish* leaves. Let us close our eyes and rest."

"Sleep? I could not close my eyes if I wanted it to. I am too stressed out. Even more nervous than you can imagine," explained Gaido, "I am literally shaking."

"Relax. Don't say another word until *The Headmaster* leaves." After a few moments of meditation, they watched Headmaster Narnish take an ornate and immaculate sword from its scabbard. As he did so, they could feel its incredible power, like it was filling up the fountain chamber with pressurized air. *Headmaster Narnish* then touched the waters of the fountain with the tip of the sword, and immediately the waters began to roil and froth like a huge cauldron over a fire. Only minutes passed when the waters settled, crystalizing into a perfect sheet of greenish glass.

"What is that sword?" asked *Mender*.

"That sword is the key to the healing waters. It is one of the Secret Treasures of the Mock Fenk Fist Kingdom. It is the Healing Sword, and always under the protection of Headmaster Narnish. No one enters the Secret Chamber where that sword is stored."

Warrior and *Mender* looked at each other and thought, "Could that be the remnant we came to Mock Fenk Fist Kingdom looking for?"

• • • • • • • •

Master Narnish performed some rituals, then submerged himself directly into the healing waters. They could only see the back of *Master Narnish*'s body, as if he were a floating corpse. But as he rose from the water, they beheld a transformation that was astonishing. He looked like a young man now, no longer frail and bent. His skin was soft and pure and his eyes were bright and hopeful. The four members in the cave tried to utter words of amazement, but *Kouken* signaled to them to be silent, drawing his thumb across his throat to convey the seriousness of the situation.

The now strong, vigorous looking man stood up and put his robe back on, readying himself to leave; he mumbled some unintelligible words that sealed the entrance of the cave.

"Well, I am glad he is gone. Have you ever seen anything like that?" exclaimed Warrior.

"You can be amazed later. I fear we are trapped in here," said Gaido.

"Let me worry about that," answered Kouken, "It is time to get *Warrior* and *Mender* into the healing waters before it's too late."

As they lowered the more seriously injured *Warrior* into the fountain, a glittering effervescence overtook him, lifting his body into the air like a cloud of light and water. As he was lowered back into the fountain, the group observed that he was completely clean. Even the blood on his shirt and trousers was gone as well.

"What strength I feel running through my veins! What power! I feel rejuvenated! I feel new! I don't feel any pain at all. I don't even feel stressed or sad. Nothing!" shouted *Warrior* at a rapid pace.

"Look at your face," said *Mender,* "Your skin looks like it is shining! It's like a baby's skin." She reached out to touch his face, almost absent mindedly. "So soft and tender. Even your hair has changed color! It's longer and softer. How handsome." They all laughed at this last little comment.

As they were getting to their feet, they heard a splash from behind them. They whirled around, unsheathing their weapons. They could not believe their eyes.

"What? I want baby's skin too," said *Mender,* sheepishly. I couldn't resist the temptation of plunging myself into this marvelous fountain. I mean, it is a once in a lifetime opportunity!" They all looked unamused. "C'mon, I was hurt too," she tried to laugh.

"Yeah right," sighed Gaido.

"Enough ogling. Now, we need to get out of here," said *Warrior,* "How are we going to escape from here?"

"It is easier than you may think," said *Kouken,* "All we have to do is wait for the first light of the sun, as the moon is just fading away. We will have a few seconds to get out when the light from both orbs mix and hit the mountain. The dawn is our way out."

Now that they knew the way out, their moods lightened, and they shared stories all night long waiting for the approaching dawn.

"Look! The moon's light is vanishing. The first ray will dart across the horizon in one or two minutes. Get ready, we only have seconds," hurried *Kouken.*

"I remember an ancient prophecy about these two warriors. You must not fight them," said *Uranaishi.*

"Are you sure? Do you know why they have come to our kingdom?" asked *Headmaster Narnish.*

"We must be wise, trusting in the prophecy. I believe they have come for the Holy Relics, at least for one of them specifically. The people of the kingdom are only aware of one Holy Relic. Only you and I know about the others. The foretelling only speaks of battle involving the two warriors and the strongest fighter in our kingdom. It doesn't mention anything about *The Headmaster* fighting them. Moreover, it is not clear who wins the battle. The book is missing some pages," said Uranaishi.

"Go, and find out the entire reasoning behind the intruders' presence in our kingdom. We must not lose anything to these trespassers," replied *Headmaster Narnish*, sternly, "There is someone, I am certain, that they will not be able to defeat my most trusted fighter, *Master Nampi.*"

CHAPTER 17

*"To another **Prophecy**. 1 Corinthians 12: 8-11"*

"It is time for you to continue your journey, finding the relic you are looking for. The secret that brought you here," said *Kouken*, "There is only one way for you to get out of this kingdom alive, possibly getting what you want as well."

"That doesn't sound very promising," said *Mender*.

"You will need to find your way into *Headmaster Narnish*'s chambers and challenge his best warrior to a fight. The pride of the warrior will allow you to bargain for your lives, and something else if you are wise enough. Of course, that is *if* you can defeat the one true warrior of this kingdom. You will need to fight *Master Nampi*. I fear for your lives. No one has ever faced him in combat, living to tell about it. There is no one like him in this kingdom. You will need to be strong and courageous to win that battle," explained *Kouken* gravely.

"What do you know about the secret relics in this kingdom, *Kouken*?" asked *Mender*.

"If by some miracle you are able to defeat *Master Nampi,* you will have the opportunity to enter *Headmaster Narnish*'s private rooms. Request one favor, and, if it is in his power, he must grant it. Insist on access to the Secret Chamber, claiming this as your prize for defeating *Nampi.* Do not be misguided. This is not an easy task. If victorious, you will be presented with five doors in the Secret Chamber. You will only have one opportunity to select the correct door. Three doors lead nowhere, and the other two doors conceal one Holy Relic each.

"The Healing Sword is one of the relics, so what is the other one?" inquired *Warrior.*

"No one has ever entered the Secret Chamber but *Headmaster Narnish* and *The Guardian of the Chamber.* Legend says that these treasures hold a great deal of power which could affect the human race immensely. You have seen one of them already," said Kouken, "That sword you saw Headmaster Narnish use earlier is *The Sword of Healing;* the other relic is known only to The Headmaster."

After a long silence, Kouken finished with, "The other mystery is the identity of the chamber's guardian, and that is also known only to *Headmaster Narnish.*"

"Interesting," murmured *Mender.*

. . . .

After they'd made their way back down the mountain, nearing the city once again, they stopped to have a more in-depth conversation regarding the relics.

"Listen," said *Kouken* directly, "They cannot discover that I am the one helping you. If you persist in using extreme caution, I will not leave you alone. Gaido will take you to the temple where you can meet *Headmaster Narnish*, and make sure you get there without further incident. Remember, do not provoke *Headmaster Narnish*. State your business clearly, and he will decide to either grant your request to fight, or have you beheaded right there," disclosed *Kouken*.

"What a relief!" exclaimed *Mender* sarcastically, "We are walking into the lion's den, where they are ready to devour us. Thank you very much, my friend, for your encouraging words."

"I've only told you the truth. Farewell for now, friends." With that *Kouken* vanished into the forest.

. . . .

As Gaido, *Mender* and *Warrior* walked along the winding path toward the city, each of them pondered what awaited them. Even though Gaido was confident in his master's plan, he could not help feeling a little uneasy. After all, they *were* heading into the heart of the lion's den. He had never had so much responsibility placed on his shoulders.

Warrior, though reinvigorated by the healing waters, was nevertheless slightly nervous. Here they were, far from home and almost completely alone. He had only narrowly escaped death a few days ago, and had it not been for the help of *Kouken* and Gaido, he would likely be in the *actual* presence of Almighty God. Also, he wasn't accustomed to accepting help or depending this long on other's. It made him feel unbalanced.

For *Mender*'s part, she was the least uneasy. She out of all of them felt the commanding presence of God, and was put at ease by His gentleness. She did feel some unrest, but it was balanced by her unmatched faith. She knew, whatever the outcome, God would deliver them.

"There it is," said Gaido.

Ahead, in the near-distance, stood the towering temple where *Nampi* and *Narnish* awaited them.

"As an aid in the temple, I can get you in and direct you to the audience chamber. From there, you'll be on your own."

"We understand," said the warriors in unison.

With that, they made their way through the inner city and up to the gate of the gorgeous, yet immense temple. The guards stationed at the main entrance allowed Gaido and his *suspects* right through.

Quickly, they converged upon the chamber door, where *Narnish* and *Nampi* were in counsel with all the masters of the kingdom.

Gaido reminded them, "This is as far as I go. Remember, don't provoke *Narnish*. For it would surely mean the end of both of you."

"Thank you, my friend," said *Mender*, bowing. Gaido returned down the stairwell.

"Here we go," was Warrior's shaky attempt at being composed.

. . . .

"Someone is approaching," hissed *Uranaishi* suspiciously.

Warrior and *Mender* pushed the huge doors wide open, revealing the massive audience chamber. Everyone in the chamber stopped, looking directly at them.

"I think you've been looking for us, haven't you boys?" beamed *Warrior*, "We've come to challenge *you*, big guy." He pointed at *Nampi* with his finger in the shape of a gun, and winked.

"So much for not provoking them," whispered *Mender* to *Warrior*.

Nampi, who had one knee up on the steps of the dais where his master was seated, had been listening to his reports. Straightening he turned to face the pair. He looked offended and amused at the same time.

"I do not recognize them. Reveal yourselves!" demanded *Nampi*.

The two warriors had been covering their faces, still wearing their disguises. With a swift motion, both *Mender* and *Warrior* whipped off the veils from their heads. The entire guard regimine immediately surrounded them, realizing who the strangers truly were. "Allow me to fight the intruders, *Headmaster Narnish*. They cannot defeat me, not in a million years," requested *Master Nampi*.

"They cannot escape this kingdom alive. You *must* kill them. They must not fulfil the purpose of their quest." *Headmaster Narnish* seethed.

Uranaishi spoke, "They are going to be killed in this battle, surely fulfilling the prophecy."

"Are you certain?" inquired *Headmaster Narnish.*

"I have seen the signs," replied *Uranaishi* reassuringly, "As long as you are not the one fighting them, we are sure to win."

"We have come to seek an audience with *Headmaster Narnish!* We are here to challenge the best fighter in your kingdom. Have him step forward, if you think he is capable of defeating us," bellowed *Mender,* in a loud and commanding voice.

"We have already defeated everyone in our path. No one has been able to escape our wrath and no one will," said *Warrior.*

Having heard this, *Master Nampi* jumped down from the steps he was kneeling on.

"What a cocky and foolhardy pair you are. I will be your opponent."

"I pledge my life on the outcome of the battle. I will win or die trying," *Nampi* said as he bowed to *The Headmaster.*

"Wait!" Boomed an incredible voice. It was *Narnish.*

"No one move a single muscle. You," he pointed at *Mender* and *Warrior,* "neither of you move, or I will wipe you from existence."

CHAPTER 18

*"To another **Discerning of spirits**. 1 Corinthians 12: 8-11"*

Tensions were high. Nobody dared to defy *Headmaster Narnish's orders.*

He continued, "What are you intruders doing in my kingdom? Speak! Before I order them to behead you."

"We came to defeat your best fighter, earning us one request in return," replied *Warrior.*

"Who do you think you are to make threats towards me? You are *nobody.* I should just have you killed right here, right now."

"We have already defeated your fighters and one of your Master's. They were no match for us. Not even your Leitai fighters stood a chance. The shame will stain your kingdom's reputation for years to come. You are renowned for being a kingdom of conquerors, a kingdom of fighters; your *Mock Fenk Fist* style is legendary," *Warrior* spoke with increased intensity, "Killing us now will only show that you are afraid of our challenge. It will be written in the eternal chronicles that two foreigners defeated the greatest fighters of this kingdom." As *Warrior* finished, he glanced over to his partner, seeing little concern in her face.

"Silence, Boy!" A fist, out of nowhere, hit *Warrior*'s face with the force of a hurricane. He hit the floor, hard, but recovered. It was *Nampi* who had dealt the devastating blow.

In a calm, but seething voice, *Narnish* spoke to *Nampi*. "I ordered that no one was to move. Not even you. *You* dare to disobey me?"

The whole chamber was as silent as a tomb. Everyone thought *Nampi* was a dead man.

Master Nampi recovered himself, realizing what he'd done. "My apologies, *Headmaster Narnish*. I just could not be still while he was disrespecting you. Let me fight them. I will honor the kingdom, avenging my pupils," said *Master Nampi*.

"Silence! I have not yet decided whether to kill them or allow them to fight you!" shouted *Narnish*. Turning to the duo, "I hope you can back up those tough words, Boy. It *would* be easier to kill you now but, then, you would not suffer for your loose tongue." He stood, slowly stepping down from his high place.

"So as not to be unfair, I will grant the both of you's wish to a battle with Master Nampi, sparing your lives, should you manage to defeat him."

Nampi grinned when he heard this.

"But, not now," was *The Headmaster*'s final statement.

"What!" shouted *Warrior* in disbelief.

"Quiet! The fact that you live, demonstrates the breadth of my magnanimity," *The Headmaster* replied, cooly.

"The great fight will take place two days from now. I will assign *Kouken* as a custodian to attend to you until then."

The Headmaster was now, speaking to the whole chamber, "Treat them as my guests! No one, and I mean, *no one* is to lay a hand on them."

Leaning in to look *Mender* and *Warrior* in the eyes, *Nampi* sneered and said,

"No, because they are mine to kill."

· · · · · · · · · · ··

"**B**ack to square one," said *Mender.*

"We have two more days to spend with you *Kouken.* It is official now, we are your guests. No more having to hide." The four of them laughed.

"Do not take this opportunity lightly. Observe and learn. You need to find a way to defeat *Master Nampi.* His weakness is his pride. I will take you to see how he trains and prepares for battle tomorrow. Watch him, and look for an opening in his fighting style. Though…" *Kouken* trailed off, "I have never seen any weaknesses, so I hope you can find one in two days."

"I think it is time to discuss the importance of your victory and retrieving the relic in order to take it back to your world." *Kouken* sat down next to *Warrior* and beckoned *Mender* to sit as well.

"*Headmaster Narnish* has been hiding the Sword of Healing within his secret chambers all these years. Are healings in your world scarce?"

Both *Mender* and *Warrior* nodded in agreement. "This is because people in your world don't believe in the Gift of Healing anymore. It has been taken away from humanity. *Headmaster Narnish* kept it hidden in Nede Land's Mock Fenk Fist kingdom, but it does not belong to us. It belongs to you, in your world."

"That is the reason there are too many sicknesses in your world. People don't rely on the Gifts of the Spirit, but more on science. You *must* retrieve it and take it back to your world and to your people. Humanity needs to believe again in the Gift of Healing"

With tears in his eyes, *Kouken* finished, "The fate of humanity is in your hands, as is the responsibility of bringing healing back to your world. We cannot do it. We are forbidden from even trying."

• • • • • • • • • • •

"**I** did not know you cared so much for the human race. I now understand perfectly why you are helping us. I was blind, but now I see," said *Mender.*

"Don't forget about me," Gaido said gently.

"Of course, you too," replied *Warrior* with a smile.

"You know, we have noticed that our Gifts of the Spirit powers work differently here than in our world."

"Of course they do. The Gifts of the Spirit are for the humanity of your world. For you to use them here, you will need to possess the sword that embodies each Gift of the Spirit. Only then, will you have the power in this kingdom. Do not despair. Power comes from your heart, from your mind and from your faith.

That is the key to winning your battle against *Master Nampi.* That and of course, finding a weak point," said *Kouken.*

"It has become clear to me now that you need special training to release your full skills when battling in Nede Land. I fear you have rushed into your death which I cannot allow. Starting early tomorrow, we will train your heart and soul. Unfortunately, we are left with only one day before the battle."

CHAPTER 19

*"To another **Different kinds of Tongues.***

1 Corinthians 12: 8-11"

Bright and early the next morning, they all decided to go and see *Master Nampi*'s training.

"I know why you've come. Watch all you want but nothing will change your fate," said *Master Nampi*, after observing *Warrior* and *Mender.* "You have rushed yourself into your doom. Enjoy your last moments in my kingdom while you still can."

Nothing good came out of observing *Master Nampi*'s training. Kouken began to despair, "We are right back where we started. I have yet to see a weak point or opening in his fighting style. *Master Nampi* is one of a kind. I am sorry, but I am beginning to lose hope that you can win," *Kouken* stated remorsefully.

"What are you saying? Don't be discouraged, we have got this," *Mender* tried with encouragement.

"You still don't get it, do you? This is not like in your world, this is Nede Land. Things are different here. Rules are not the same," Kouken said defiantly, "Enough with all of this."

He waved his hand casually, forcing a smile, "Let us enjoy your last moments together."

"Geeze. Encouraging words. Was that your idea of a pep talk?" added Gaido.

"Well, yes," *Kouken* said sheepishly. They all laughed heartily.

"They spent a full day of training, learning new techniques and moves. Completely exhausting themselves, they began to accept what they believed was the inevitable plan God had for them. They decided to stroll through the town that night, trying to relax themselves, before the impending fight the next day. It was the first time *Warrior* was able to walk in the open, and see the kingdom.

"This is really beautiful. So peaceful and calm. The people seem happy too," observed *Warrior*.

"I am glad you had the chance to see it as I had," said *Mender*. The sun began descending into a bath of ruddy and sultry colors, brushing the stones of the walkway and walls of the houses in ruby and gold. As they walked, villagers were observed shutting up their doors, lighting candles and sitting down with their families.

"I think we should head home now, before it gets dark," said *Kouken*.

Walking towards their quarters, they pondered the future.

.

"Did anybody notice someone following us?" observed *Warrior*, "He is out in the open, a hundred steps back, and not even trying to go unnoticed."

"Should we confront him," said Gaido.

"Or *her,*" corrected *Mender*.

"Sorry," said Gaido.

"It is ok," comforted *Mender*.

"I do not think that is necessary. No one will dare to attack the *Headmaster Narnish*'s guests," remarked *Kouken*.

They arrived home to *Kouken*'s place, and were ready to pass out. Knock… knock… knock…

Three hard, deliberate knocks.

Kouken went to the door, opening it. Were his eyes deceiving him?

"Old man! I cannot believe you are here. I thought you passed away years ago," *Kouken* bursted with joy and astonishment.

"I thought I would never see this day," began the old man,"I have been waiting for years for this day. I thought death was going to catch me before I accomplished my task."

"Accomplishing *your* task? Hum!" *Kouken* jested.

The old man spied *Mender* and *Warrior,* "Ah! These must be the legendary fighters."

"*Legendary?* I think you are confusing us with some other warriors, old man," *Mender* said, provoking laughter from *Warrior.*

The old man sat down and took a long draught from the pale water.

"As by now you know, there is an ancient prophecy here in Mock Fenk Fist kingdom, and I am here to help you fulfill it."

The old man went further into detail about the legend that spoke of a warrior from another land, "I was confused at first because the books spoke of *the chosen one*. Naturally, I was expecting only one warrior, but two is better," said the old man.

"Who are you, old man?" *Warrior* asked.

Gaido abruptly interrupted, saying, "He is none other than the *MASTER* of *Master Nampi*. The legendary warrior who was once the King of this fair land. After the succession of the new King, Headmaster Narnish, he vanished. Everyone thought he died. No one dared to speak his name, and why everyone calls him the "old man.""

"Your *Highness*," said Gaido, bowing before the former monarch.

"Stop that, Gaido. We don't have time for any of your silliness. Besides, that's part of my past. We'll have time to catch up later. Right now, I am here because of them." He turned to *Warrior* and *Mender*. "Look here, you two. You cannot defeat *Nampi*. I trained him and he was the only one I ever knew who would go to absolutely any lengths to win a battle. You must yield if you wish to live."

"NEVER!" shouted *Warrior* and *Mender* as one.

"I hoped you would say that. Allow me to share one short story to enlighten you all. In all my years of training *Nampi*, he was constantly growing and growing. I had him face all kinds of opponents, stronger than him in every way. Yet, every time he came out victorious. When fighting battles for the kingdom, he was fearless. There was not a single battle that he could not win. As his reputation and strength grew, so did his *pride*.

"One day, I was meditating when he came to me. He wanted to show me his strength in battle. I accepted and we fought for only five minutes. He was equal to me in every way. I could feel he was stronger than I was, but then I saw a crack in his facade. A glimpse was all I had. A sliver of an opening. It was not in his fighting style or technique, it was his arrogance. He was convinced that he was stronger than I was, and could defeat me. That is his moment of carelessness."

They were all listening very carefully, grasping the lesson behind it.

The old man spoke quietly, "There is only one way to make him show you that vulnerability. He must see that he can defeat you. When he thinks it is all over for you in the battle, in that split second, you will see the opening. But, if you miss it, the end for you two will be unavoidable."

CHAPTER 20

*"To another **The Interpretation of Tongues.***
1 Corinthians 12: 8-11"

Since first light, people had been funneling into the square to observe the fight, until nearly everyone in the kingdom was there.

"This is a big day, a historic day," said *Kouken*, "Most of the people in the kingdom have never seen the great *Master Nampi* in a real battle." He passed his hand over the crowd in a sweeping gesture. "They are all here to watch him fight. They are not here because they want you out of the kingdom. That is only a secondary concern to the people."

"Woo! This really is a crazy kingdom!" cried *Warrior*.

The crowd was a roar of activity. Farmers, merchants, blacksmiths, fisherman and every other kind of producer had taken the day to witness this landmark event. Fighters from all the schools and their masters were gathered as well, hoping to observe the legendary skill of *Master Nampi* for themselves.

Vendors, poets, entertainers and scribes were among the crowd. Taking advantage of the huge numbers of onlookers, by performing their art and trading their wares. It was as if an entirely new town within the capital had formed, so dense and lively was the population of spectators.

Suddenly, a divide began to form in the crowd leading up to the arena. It was *Headmaster Narnish,* walking with a contingent of his finest warriors and guardsmen. As he ascended to the podium, a hush fell over the crowd.

"It is time for the preliminary rituals and ceremonies to begin! Bring the challengers here before me," he boomed with his powerful voice. The crowd started yelling and screaming then.

"*Nampi! Nampi! Nampi!*" in a single resounding voice. The whole of the kingdom shouted the name of their champion.

The rituals and ceremonies were more like a celebration, and lasted over an hour. It was tradition to lead the contenders around the arena on a mobile stage fixed to a team of horses, allowing the crowd to cheer or jeer depending on their mood. This was also an opportunity for the fighters to wave and salute their fans, if they had any. Though these particular fighters were not fond of one another, they were expected to show respect, standing side by side for the entire ceremony.

It was apparent, however, that the crowd only wanted to see the fight. They grew weary of the ceremony and began to chant at a deafening volume, "Fight, fight, fight, fight!"

The Headmaster regained control of the crowd and spoke again, "Ladies and gentlemen! It is time for you to see what you came here to see! Our best warrior, the one and only *Master Nampi* will represent the excellence of our kingdom. Behold! The almighty *Master Nampi!*"

With the announcement of his name, the crowd erupted into a fury of cheers. They threw confetti and sloshed their drinks into the air, until it was alive with a riot of color. Master Nampi bowed, and then with a grand gesture, unsheathed his sword and thrust his arms into the air with a mighty roar. He had complete command of the crowd. It was a spectacle that defies description, and neither *Warrior* nor Mender had ever seen anything like it before in their lives.

Headmaster Narnish slowly raised his hand, calling for silence. "The rules are simple. If you defeat *Master Nampi*, you will not only be allowed to walk out of here alive, but I will also grant you one wish, upon my honor. That is, if you manage to defeat my fighter, which we all know will never happen." The crowd laughed uncontrollably.

Headmaster Narnish waited for the crowd's laughter to die down before commanding, "Let the battle begin!"

The fighters were directed to the ring, and separated to their respective corners. *Nampi* drew his sword with a cavalier flourish, as if to signify his utter contempt for his opponents. *Warrior* and *Mender* transformed into their bejeweled black armor, readying themselves for the fight of their lives.

The bell rang, and *Nampi* disappeared in a blur. The pair had no time to react, they simply braced for the first blows. Oh, what a mighty blows from their opponent! With almost no time between attacks, they were both struck, barely deflecting anything with their swords. *Nampi* was flying around the arena, then circled back for another attack.

The second pass presented what they thought was an opening, but it was a fake. *Nampi* predicted they'd take his bait, and he laughed, as he parried their combined attack, throwing them across the arena with a swing of his sword.

"Man, nothing is working on this guy," groaned *Warrior*, "How long has it been?"

Mender chuckled, "Forty seconds."

"Great," said *Warrior* sarcastically, "*Mender*, we have to use everything we've got on this guy, and I mean now."

Mender was busy dodging devilishly fast sword swipes that *Warrior* hadn't even detected. "I'm open to suggestions!" she shouted.

Warrior attempted to back her up, but blow after blow, they were thrashed and thrown around like ragdolls.

At the end of the first five minutes, the pair was already severely injured, edging closer to death. In the back of their minds, they had been holding on to the hope that there would be an opening in *Master Nampi*'s technique. They knew it would be their only chance, but that moment didn't appear to be coming.

"*Mender!*" cried out *Warrior*, as he saw her tossed to the ground, unconscious and unable to move. He did not know if she was still breathing or not.

Nampi landed on his feet right next to *Warrior* with an awful thump that shook the ground. *Warrior* was on his knees, retching up blood and breathing heavily. He looked up to see *Nampi* with an evil smile on his face.

"Your partner is finished. Now, it is your time to die, Boy. Where is that strength you were talking about? Show me a real battle! Give me the kind of fight you showed all the others!" *Nampi* kicked *Warrior* savagely in the ribs. "You like that? Let me show you my real strength!"

He proceeded to kick *Warrior* repeatedly, juggling him into the air, landing a final kick to the solar plexus that was so devastating, it made *Warrior* swear he saw Heaven itself.

Transported to an ethereal plane of mist and light, *Warrior*'s head swam with thoughts and feelings.

"Am I dreaming or already dead?" In the distance, after an unknown span of time, he heard a voice echoing off the infinite landscape.

Wake up!

Get up!

Don't give up!

You can make it!

As his sight returned to the mortal plane, he heard a sinister voice saying,

"Wake up. Time to die." *Nampi* had picked him up by the collar of his armor.

"Say your last words, Boy."

He did not know how, but as *Nampi* raised his fist as if to cave in *Warrior*'s skull, his unconscious mind and body dodged the blow, rolling out of immediate danger.

"Oh, got a little fight left in you, eh?" teased *Nampi.*

Nampi appeared to be stalling, but he was ready to finish the fight.

"Honestly I cannot understand how you are still standing. You have endured more than anyone who has ever fought against me, and I will honor your bravery, by finishing you quickly!" *Master Nampi* disappeared once more into a whirlwind of speed and ferocity.

Warrior was lost in his thoughts for a moment. Feeling like hours, but it was just a fraction of a second that had passed. I *swear I saw Mender winking at me,* he thought.

This time, clear as day, he saw *Mender* wink again. She was not dead! It looked as if she discovered something while lying on the ground like that.

In his mind he heard her voice.

Warrior, this is our only chance! I have seen his weakness. If we miss it, we will fail at accomplishing our tasks. Fusion is the only way to finish him.

Their spirits and minds became as one, as their strengths melded together. That very moment, *Nampi* descended, making his final blow. Screaming with a terrible quake, shaking the ground with a thunder-clap, the duo fell, motionless.

The crowd, stunned for an instant by what they witnessed, erupted moments later in a cheer of victorious glee.

"*NAMPI!*" they shouted.

Apparently satisfied with himself, *Nampi* strode lazily over to the winner's circle, amid showers of applause and flower petals.

"I expected nothing less from you, *Master Nampi*. It took you longer than I thought it would, but you are victorious." *Headmaster Narnish* touched *Nampi* on the shoulder in a gesture of congratulations. "You have done well, and we are proud of you. As always, you have shown yourself to be my worthy successor."

When *Headmaster Narnish* removed his hand from *Nampi's* shoulder, the glorified master stammered,

"I did well, didn't I?" Seemingly, in a daze he began to fall backward. *Nampi's* eyes went wide and glossed over as he fell to the ground at *Narnish's* feet, stone dead.

"What... has... happened...? How... is ... this... possible...? This cannot be happening." *Narnish* was dumbstruck.

When *Headmaster Narnish* looked over into the square, expecting to see two dead challengers, both *Mender* and *Warrior* were alive and standing triumphantly. Confused and speechless by the outcome of the battle, *Headmaster Narnish* started walking away. Warrior shouted after him,

"We defeated your champion! We get one wish, remember?"

"You are free to walk out of here today, alive. We will settle the matter of your wish tomorrow. Today is now a day of mourning," he replied somberly.

CHAPTER 21

"But one and the same Spirit works all these things, distributing to each one individually as He wills 1 Corinthians 12: 8-11"

The following day, *Narnish* held an audience with the two who defeated his champion. In the audience chamber with his advisor, he beckoned the duo step forward.

"What is it you want?" he scowled with no small amount of disdain.

"We want access to your Secret Chamber."

"I told you they were coming for the treasures," *Uranaishi* said to *Narnish*.

"Remember the prophecy, Sire," whispered *Uranaishi* into *Headmaster Narnish*'s ear.

"Very well then, I will take you there."

Narnish led them behind his throne and through a secret tunnel beneath the temple. As they wound their way down through the bowels of the earth, it became cold and dank, demonstrating clearly that they were very deep.

"This is the Secret Chamber of Treasures; no one has ever set foot in here but The Guardian and myself. *You* will be the first in all the ages. There are five doors, you must choose only one. Behind three of the doors you find nothing but air, but the other two conceal one secret treasure each. If you select one of the doors that is empty, you will find yourselves facing *The Guardian*."

Mender and *Warrior* began to think. They had observed *The Headmaster* carefully while he explained the dilemma to them. In his motions and tone there were no clues. Upon two of the doors there was an inscription, something they could not understand, and was of no help either. *Mender* noticed that one of the doors was a slightly more polished than the others, as if someone had kept it clean.

"*Warrior*, let us have faith and pick this one." *Mender* pointed to the polished door.

Before they could open the door, *Headmaster Narnish* said,

"Wait! Are you sure that is the door you want?"

"Yes, we are," said *Warrior* confidently, looking back to *Mender*.

When they opened the door, a bright light leapt from the center of the chamber. The light was an otherworldly, pale green, reminding them of the healing waters.

They approached and saw an incredible sword, luminous and ornate. Upon the pedestal where it rested were the words:

Gift of Healing

Warrior and *Mender* grabbed the sword at the same time and began walking out of the chamber with their treasure.

They were able to rescue and secure the hidden treasure. Held securely in their hands was the *Gift of Healing*. Once returned to their world, it would initiate humanity's ability to receive and believe in the healing powers of the Holy Spirit.

• • • • • • • ••

*H*eadmaster *Narnish* knew he could not say nor do anything about it. They were holding true power in their hands, even if they did not know its true potential. But he was not hopeless, he still had an ace up his sleeve. *Uranaishi* and *Headmaster Narnish*'s were still hiding something more powerful than that sword, behind one of the other doors in the chamber. But, they were not going to share it with anyone. That was *their* secret to keep; after all, they are *The Guardians* and protectors of the *Malsi* Group.

Dear Reader,

I hope you enjoyed the first books in the series: *The Hero Within: Awareness & The Hero Within: Power.*

I have to tell you, I really love this hero story. Many readers wrote me asking, "What's next for our Hero?" Well, be sure to stay tuned because the saga of publishing Christian Fiction isn't quite over. Our Hero will be back in book four. Will he have more power? I sure hope so.

When I wrote *The Hero Within: Nede Land 1;* I got many letters from fans thanking me for the books. Some had opinions about the adventures, while others simply rooted for Babul Ell.

As an author, I love feedback. Candidly, you're the reason I will explore the Hero's future. So tell me what you liked, what you loved, even what you hated. You can write to me at comments@christianhero.org and visit me on the web at www.christianhero.org.

Finally, I need to ask a favor. If you're so inclined, I'd love a review of *The Hero Within: Nede Land 1*. Loved it, hated it—I'd just enjoy your feedback.

Reviews can be tough to come by these days, and you, the reader, have the power to make or break a book. If you have the time, ***here's a link to my author page, along with all my books on Amazon: http://amzn.to/19p3dNx***

Thank you so much for reading *The Hero Within: Nede Land 1* and for spending time with me.

In gratitude,

Yeral E. Ogando

Yeral E. Ogando comes from a very humble origin and continues to be a humble servant of our Lord Almighty; understanding that we are nothing but vessels and the Lord who called us, also sends us to do His work, not our work. *Luke 17:10 "So likewise ye, when ye shall have done all those things which are commanded you, say, We are*

unprofitable servants: we have done that which was our duty to do."

Mr. Ogando was born in the Caribbean, Dominican Republic. He is the beloved father of two beautiful girls "Yeiris & Tiffany" and three handsome boys "Bennett, Ethan & Nathan"

Jesus brought him to His feet at the age of 16-17. Since then, he has served as Co-pastor, pastor, Bible School teacher, youth counselor, and church planter.

Fluent in several languages Mr. Ogando is the Creator and owner of an Online Translation Ministry operating since 2007; with Native Christian translators in more than 25 countries and translating into more than 250 languages. (www.christian-translation.com),

The most exciting thing about his Translation Ministry is that thousands of people are receiving the Word of God in their native language on a daily basis and hundreds of ministries are able to reach the world through the work of Christian-Translation.com along with his network of websites in different languages related to Christian Translation and Christian Services.

He's earned several degrees among them: Master of Arts in Theological Studies, Master of Arts in Languages and Linguistics and Doctor of Philosophy in Theology.

I would like you to share with me your impression and / or ideas after reading my books. Feel free to email them to me at comments@christianhero.org. It would be my honor to hear your thoughts about **The Hero Within Saga**.

1. What part of the story did you like the most?

2. What part of the story did you like the least?

3. Which one was your favorite character and why?

4. What have you learned after reading the series?

5. *There is a secret message behind most of the names, but only by using your imagination, you will decode them.* Which ones were you able to decode?

6. Which ones were the hardest to decode?

7. What is your general impression on the books?

8. What do you expect to happen next and what would you like to happen? *I will surely take your ideas into consideration and if they are good enough, I will definitely mention your name when taking them into consideration.*

9. Finally, Make sure to check the Manga version at www.christianhero.org

By completing this challenge properly, you are entering **The Hero Within Challenge**. We will select 10 winners with different prizes. Make sure to state that you want to participate in **The Hero Within Challenge** when sending your feedback form.